FELSTEAD

FELSTEAD

Kay Stephens

This edition first published in Great Britain 1996 by
SEVERN HOUSE PUBLISHERS LTD of
9–15 High Street, Sutton, Surrey SM1 1DF.
First published in the USA 1996 by
SEVERN HOUSE PUBLISHERS INC. of
595 Madison Avenue, New York, NY 10022.

British Library Cataloguing in Publication Data

Stephens, Kay
    Felstead
    1. English fiction – 20th century
    I. Title
    823.9′14 [F]

    ISBN 0-7278-4961-1

Typeset by Palimpsest Book Production Limited,
Polmont, Stirlingshire, Scotland.
Printed and bound in Great Britain by
Hartnolls Ltd, Bodmin, Cornwall.

FELSTEAD

Chapter One

A lone sea gull wheeled majestically, soaring phantom-white against a sky darkened to indigo by the threatening storm. Jay shivered as the gull's keening cry pierced the thrumming of the Lancia's engine. It was Good Friday afternoon—a time which no amount of rationalizing could dissociate from death.

She reached the top of the gradient and sighed. The house was visible already—a gaunt mansion dominating the moor, its blackened York sandstone as forbidding as the surrounding sky. Wryly, she smiled. Paul had warned her that Rhys Felstead was no more welcoming than his house; whatever this Easter brought, she'd expect no joy.

Jay was accustomed to the reluctance with which she was taken into a home. Being an art expert frequently involved breaking the news that someone's treasured painting was worth far less than they'd supposed. This time, the authenticity of seven paintings was in question, and Rhys Felstead would reject anything but incontrovertible proof that they were faked.

Hailstones rattled on the windshield as she drove over the straight road leading to Scree Carr. The icy particles were hurled toward her like a deterrent and again Jay smiled, though again she shivered. She needed no elements to reinforce her longing to be somewhere else. But for Paul's insistence, she'd have opposed Mr. Felstead's wish that she spend Easter here.

His telephone call had been terse, a command intimating that if Paul Valentine valued the opportunity to auction the Felstead collection, he would send someone immediately to prove or disprove that these seven pictures were forged. And so Jay was the victim.

Victim wasn't ordinarily the way she'd describe herself. Having studied, feverishly acquiring knowledge, until she equaled and then surpassed most men of similar age in her field, she wasn't readily deterred. At present, though, she *was* exhausted. It had been nearly a year since the terminal illness through which she had nursed her mother, yet somehow, Jay hadn't managed to throw off the lingering weariness.

Paul had been more than good to her. Spending time that he could ill-spare from expanding the business, he'd wined and dined her in fashionable restaurants in and around London. They'd visited Paris and the States, mingling business with pleasure, easing their occupational pressures together, in romantic surroundings.

It wasn't Paul's fault that Jay had been unable to unwind and let the atmosphere take effect; he'd been patient, even when she couldn't explain why she didn't respond to him. They were more than friends, after all. They were companions as well as associates; the fact that their relationship went no further was an enigma to Jay herself as much as to Paul.

The heavy iron gates set in a high stone wall seemed implacable. Hauling up the collar of her fur coat against the driving hail, Jay impatiently stepped from the car. As if triggered by some secret release, the gates swung open while she was still four or five paces away.

Returning hurriedly to the car, Jay drove through, sensing, ridiculously, that they might close just as inexplicably. A movement drew her glance sideways to a compact cottage in the lee of the wall. At its window an impassive old man raised a respectful hand in brief salute before he pressed the electric button, closing the gates behind her.

The house she approached was three-storied, solid as the Yorkshire folk who had fashioned it centuries ago. In summer the extensive gardens might soften its glowering appearance. Today, with hailstones whitening out the contours of flower beds and lawns and the storm inking out yew hedges and shrubs, Jay felt the place was drained of color as well as warmth.

The front entrance was imposing, with solid mahogany doors beyond a portico reached by a flight of stone steps. But the windows to either side and above the door seemed as bleak as the landscape, empty and cold.

Jay left the car hastily, dismissing her reluctance, as she raised her shoulders and straightened her spine. She breathed deeply and evenly, preparing herself for the encounter with Mrs. Godfrey, the housekeeper. From Paul's description, the woman was as dour as her master.

The doorbell surprised her, its tone melodic, far removed from the clanging she'd anticipated. Her second surprise came when the door was opened, not by the woman, but by a lean elegant male whose spectacles failed to mask the most penetrating brown eyes she'd ever seen.

"Miss Stanmer?"

"Yes." Jay found she couldn't say more.

"Rhys Felstead." He did not offer to shake her hand, but motioned her through. Jay felt irrationally that she was being snared.

"I'll take your bag." He extended a hand for her case. "My housekeeper is away, but you won't be uncomfortable. My daily woman comes in to clean and cook. If anything fails to satisfy, you need only say."

The icily formal words, delivered as he led the way briskly to the staircase, were devoid of any warmth.

He opened a door on the first floor and indicated that she should enter.

"I trust you will be comfortable," he said, still coolly indifferent. "You'll wish to freshen up after your journey. Dinner will be at eight."

And that appeared to be that. He set her case inside the door and disappeared, his retreating feet inaudible on the thickly carpeted landing. Paul certainly hadn't exaggerated. Surely any other host would have shown her the bathroom or explained how to find the dining room when she was permitted to emerge from her room.

Jay glanced around, admitting that the room was very beautiful—the ideal sanctuary for an art connoisseur. The dark paneled walls were a good foil for the lovingly restored oil paintings. She identified a Constable, one of Turner's most appealing sunsets, and a Reynolds portrait. There could be no doubting their authenticity, and the five or six lesser works seemed equally genuine. But then, she supposed Rhys Felstead wouldn't place anything less in the room that could be scrutinized at leisure by someone of her experience. Whatever one might accuse him of, it wouldn't be stupidity.

The walls were hung also with a large tapestry

depicting a battle scene, and three gilt-framed mirrors, the largest facing the bed, were set between huge windows from which icy drafts penetrated.

The windows were curtained with heavy brocade which, although obviously not antique, had been carefully chosen to complement the room. Jay smiled to herself. Rhys Felstead could justly claim to be artistic. No matter how lovely the room, however, it was terribly cold; Jay hurried toward the open grate where logs blazed.

Crossing the carpet, she noticed a door standing ajar and found it led to a bathroom. Once she'd unpacked the few belongings that she'd brought, she intended to take a leisurely bath. Everything indicated that she was in for a tough weekend, and she had to face it with every possible advantage.

While hanging up garments and setting out makeup, hairbrush, and comb, Jay noted that, as with everything in here, the furniture appeared well chosen and expensive. The mahogany surfaces gleamed like newly purchased reproductions, yet she recognized them as genuine Regency pieces.

Jay was drying herself in the enormous cold bathroom when someone rapped on the bedroom door; donning her robe, she hastened to open it.

Rhys Felstead was standing there. He looked briefly embarrassed at bringing her to the door, but instead of apology his voice was heavy with rebuke.

"I see you have left your car at the front entrance. Didn't Manners tell you where to garage it?"

"Manners?"

"At the lodge. The old fool's becoming incompetent—"

"Perhaps he didn't realize who I was."

"Of course he knew, I advised him of your arrival. I

don't encourage casual visitors. However, will you kindly place your car in one of the garages to the rear as soon as you're dressed?"

"Certainly," Jay responded tersely, resenting his reproving tone.

Instead of dressing hastily, she deliberately took her time, brushing her long blond hair until it gleamed, swirling it high at the back of her head, then anchoring it with an antique gold clasp. And she went downstairs only when she was ready for dinner. She may be here at his request, but she'd show Mr. Rhys Felstead she wasn't obliged to suffer his heavy-handedness.

They met in the echoing entrance hall as she crossed toward the front door, and Jay felt his piercing brown eyes assessing her appearance.

She was wearing a mid-calf dress of a soft blue woolen material, and anticipated another rebuke for not dressing for dinner. She glanced toward him, observed that he himself was wearing nothing more formal than a perfectly tailored lounge suit, and raised her gray eyes challengingly.

Astonishingly, the eyes behind the lenses seemed briefly to glint with amusement, and he gave a tiny snort that might have been laughter.

"You evidently are not aware of the severity of our North Country climate, Miss Stanmer. We don't venture outside without some protection."

About to turn and fetch her coat, she felt a surprisingly gentle hand on her arm. "There's no need—here, use this."

He grasped a heavy sheepskin jacket from a nearby hook and then held it out for her. "I know it won't fit, but it'll prevent your catching pneumonia while you walk back from the garage."

"Thank you," Jay murmured, feeling rather awkward as she thrust her arms into its sleeves, then caught the coat about her. But when she turned to smile her acknowledgment, he was striding away from her.

The evening air was cold, although the hail had passed and the last traces of white had melted from the lawns. Jay started the car, puzzling over which way around the house she was supposed to go. Her headlights showed that the drive circled the building, so perhaps the direction was immaterial.

Halfway around the side of the house, she met a blank wall. Sighing heavily, she turned the car in the opposite direction. This time she made her way to the rear of the house, and was confronted with triple garage doors. She was wondering which door to try when, possibly activated by some photoelectric cell, one of the doors began to rise. She smiled, despite herself; whatever his circumstances, Rhys Felstead denied himself no modern gadgetry.

After locking her car and securing the garage door, Jay drew up the collar of the coat, hugging it around her against the bitter cold. The moonlight revealed that this side of the estate was fenced, and the wind rushed toward her as if it came over vast arctic wastes.

Moonlight appeared to be the only illumination here; surprised that no lights shone from any of the rooms, Jay stepped back and glanced up. She shuddered, so chilled that the thick sheepskin failed to warm her. Above and to either side of the garages, every window had been boarded over.

Finding her way to the front without light took a while, and Jay suspected her host had meant her to experience some difficulty. He was still standing beside the fire in the hall, holding a whisky tumbler and sipping pensively. He scrutinized her as she entered.

"You took your time," he remarked sharply.

"Thanks for the loan of your coat," Jay said, returning it to its hook. "You were right, it was much colder than I imagined."

"I would have expected that you might have hurried then."

"You didn't tell me which way to go," she observed, her tone as sharp as his. "And a flashlight might have come in handy."

He made no comment. "Sherry?" he inquired, sounding reluctant.

"No, it doesn't matter, thank you. You seem anxious to dine."

The dining room was splendid, its imposing furniture old, well-preserved oak. The sideboard was carved, matching the heavy backs of the chairs ranged along both sides and at either end of the long table.

"This is beautiful," Jay remarked, and momentary pleasure warmed his dark eyes before he glanced away. He took the carver chair at the head of the table, and Jay sat to his right, feeling thankful he hadn't sent her to the farthest end.

"You have excellent taste." She admired the gold candelabra, wine coolers, and salvers which vied for brilliance with the delicately cut crystal goblets. Ruby-red velvet curtains shifted in the draft from the windows.

"This furniture is original, almost as old as the house, unlike the pieces in the room you're using, which were purchased later by an ancestor."

"Everything seems perfectly chosen, to create a composite picture."

"One tries," Rhys said coldly.

Jay wished he would unbend a little in response to her very real appreciation. They both liked beautiful things; couldn't they make that their common ground?

A neat little woman in a dark dress served soup that was welcomingly hot and delicately flavored with herbs. As Rhys passed Jay the crusty bread rolls, she decided she had to try to establish some sort of rapport with him.

"I imagine you're reluctant to admit a stranger to assess some of your possessions," she began, trying to smile sympathetically.

He appeared surprised and shrugged. "I need to know if the pictures in question have any real value." He hesitated. "But yes, I do resent that need—you understand why I can't welcome you."

If not why you must adopt a coolness that borders on being rude, Jay thought, then stifled the thought, trying to establish some cordiality.

"Was one of your antecedents anxious to evade window tax?" she asked.

"No." The word was rapped out, and his eyes behind the glasses were veiled. Jay couldn't imagine why he was perturbed by such an innocent question.

"But all the windows to the rear have been boarded over."

"That's not your concern," Rhys snapped.

"I'll keep my thoughts to myself then," she hissed back. The man really was impossible. Did his loathing of the situation excuse his determination to make her hate every moment of her stay?

She felt him gazing at her again, but kept her attention on the soup, thankful it was good. If the rest of the food was as superb, she would have one thing for which she could feel grateful.

"Wine?" he invited, his voice warming as he reached for her glass.

"Please."

"I hope that you drink red. I assure you this is excellent."

"I'm sure it will be." Jay matched her cool tone to his own.

"I try to compensate, in the quality of what I provide, for any shortcomings in the way it's offered," he said smoothly—so smoothly that Jay wondered if she could really have heard correctly.

She was compelled to look at him. Rhys smiled, if ruefully. "You see, I'm not unaware of your thoughts, but I don't apologize. I believe I'm old enough for people to take me as I am—or *not*, if they prefer."

"You don't care what anybody thinks of you, do you?" she exclaimed.

"Should I?"

The question was unanswerable. Jay glanced down at her plate and was relieved when the daily woman came in with their second course.

"How soon can I see the paintings?" she inquired, anxious to find some topic that wouldn't invoke further perturbing answers.

"Is after our meal soon enough? Are you so eager to escape?"

Checking the impulse to echo the word took all her willpower. Had she made her uneasiness so obvious? And was he enjoying the fact?

Rhys laughed wryly. "You needn't pretend. When Paul Valentine was here, he didn't trouble to disguise his feelings. I can't imagine he failed to warn you of the atmosphere."

Jay swallowed hard, but somehow could not conceal her smile.

"Ah." He was gazing intently at her, and their eyes met.

"Do you enjoy making people uncomfortable?" Jay asked quietly.

"I don't expect enjoyment from life, Miss Stanmer, nor, as we've established already, from this situation."

She controlled a sigh. There was no point in pursuing this discussion, or any other. Rhys was determined to be abrasive.

They scarcely spoke again during the meal. Feeling infinitely relieved, Jay followed when he rose and indicated a door at the end of the room. Making their way along corridors and up stairs, Rhys detoured at intervals to show her his most-prized paintings.

By the time they reached a door at the end of a corridor on the upper story, Jay had realized he must be one of the wealthiest men in the country.

"All the pictures in doubt are in this one room; I'll leave you here to examine them. I realize you'll need a more detailed examination in daylight, but take as long as you wish over this preliminary inspection."

Rhys was holding the door ajar for her, and Jay was forced to pass close to him as she went through. She experienced a fierce pull of attraction, which was alarming because she'd found nothing attractive in his manner.

He reached around her to switch on a light, his brown eyes seeking hers. The faintest of smiles hovered over his thin lips. He knew what she'd felt.

"Thank you," she said coldly. "I'll be glad to take my time here."

The door closed behind him. Breathing rapidly, Jay had to exert conscious effort to regain control. She'd never met a man more calculated to aggravate. She would make certain she did a thorough job. Paul had spoken of giving her the position in New York if she impressed him here, but once she'd finished she would leave at the earliest possible instant.

The paintings were unquestionably good; she could see why Rhys had believed they were genuine. Even after prolonged examination, Jay admitted that if Paul hadn't suggested they might be faked, she wouldn't immediately have doubted their authenticity. But she knew she had to be methodical in supporting her verdict, and that would require more time than she would like to spend here.

After scrutinizing each painting, she glanced about the room and was surprised to find it was a bedroom. The bed, a four-poster, had dustcovers draped over the mattress, but otherwise the room appeared ready for occupation. The place felt eerie, though, its corners shadowy, the dark curtains clinging to the carpet so that they were caught away from the windows leaving room to conceal anything. Or anyone. But worse than that was the pervading disquiet.

Inexplicably apprehensive, Jay glanced toward the paintings, stacked by the panelled walls. She'd intended to begin itemizing the data supporting her conclusions, but now she knew remaining in the room would be unbearable. Feeling claustrophobic, she ached to let in the moonlight.

An owl hooted and she jumped. She silently reproved herself for being ridiculous as she crossed to draw aside the curtains.

Jay gasped. Beyond the panes of glass was a wall of wooden planks that had been nailed across.

"I didn't bring you here to inspect my home, Miss Stanmer."

Rhys's angry voice startled her and she whipped around.

"I was just wondering how much light there'd be in here tomorrow."

"Were you?" He'd seen through her excuse, and Jay sensed he would be dangerous if antagonized—yet why should she fear him?

Sardonically, he ambled toward another set of windows on the opposite wall. Drawing back their curtains, he indicated the moonlight beyond.

"You see—you needn't be afraid. There'll be ample light for your work." He laughed, astonishing her. "And if you come here again at night, you'll be able to reassure yourself by a glimpse of open country."

This time his laughter had sounded different, sympathetic. Jay looked at him. Slowly, he smiled.

"If you don't like the room, that'll be good reason to complete the job speedily."

"You needn't worry, I won't waste time here. I'll be gone soon, and then you'll be happy."

"Happy?" he echoed. "Is that what you think?"

Jay understood that he was anything but happy here—and that he wanted to make her aware of the fact, but his emotions were no concern of hers.

"I'm sure you won't mind if I have an early night now," she said.

"Not in the least. This way . . ."

At the door of her room, Rhys gave a curt little bow. "I chose the shortest route; I'd hate to get you lost."

"Do people get lost here?" she asked lightly. "The house is large, isn't it, and the layout is confusing."

"What makes you think that anyone would come here?"

Without saying good night, he turned away abruptly and disappeared through a door across the landing from her own.

Jay undressed slowly, disturbed—and annoyed because she was sure her host wanted to disturb her. Why on earth should he care what she felt about his home, or about anything?

She was still conscious of the drafts stirring the curtains and the wind in the chimney, but someone had banked up the fire. She was as grateful for the cheer of its blaze as for the warmth.

Wearing her nightgown and housecoat, Jay sat on the hearth rug, marshaling her thoughts to make notes.

Somehow, though, her mind persisted in wandering to her enigmatic host instead of the paintings. She laid aside her notebook and crossed quickly to the bed.

The mattress was comfortable, the covers were adequate, but Jay found sleep elusive. Unaccustomed to light in her bedroom, the glowing fire obtruded, and its crackling logs threatened to keep her awake all night by spitting each time she was on the verge of sleep.

Other noises increased her restlessness. The house itself creaked and groaned in the way old houses will, and beyond her window tree branches sighed in the wind, tapping intermittently on the glass. She became aware of the ticking of the antique clock which earlier she'd thought exquisite. And over the identifiable sounds she noticed a curious rushing noise that reminded her of the sea, and puzzled her because she was certain they were nowhere near the coast.

Eventually, closing her eyes and pulling the covers over her ears, Jay willed herself to ignore everything and to sleep. She need spend only a few nights at Scree Carr. Feeling disturbed wouldn't harm her.

She was awakened while it was still dark, terrified by dreadful cries. Even while she lay trembling, wondering if she'd been dreaming, she heard the moaning again and shuddered. The anguish was so intense, it made her feel sick with anxiety. Again, she listened. Was it some animal, injured, out on the moors? A snared fox perhaps?

The next time she heard the sounds, she realized they were much nearer than she'd first thought. Had some creature strayed into the house and become trapped? The cry seemed a terrified one.

There was no way that she could lie there and let that sound continue. The logs had died to ash in the hearth, leaving her room totally dark. Never more desperate for light, she felt toward the bedside lamp.

Thrusting on her housecoat, Jay opened the door but then stopped abruptly. Another despairing cry echoed through the walls, and it came from the room across from her own—the room that was Rhys Felstead's.

Without pausing to think, Jay sped to rescue whatever or whoever was in that room with him. She flung open the door and stood on the threshold, the glimmer of light from her own doorway revealing only the first few yards of carpeted floor and an armchair, its back toward her.

It occurred to her then that Rhys might have been attacked by an intruder. She wiped sticky palms down her robe and felt for the light switch.

The only occupant of the room was her host himself. The upper part of his body was uncovered and bare. He was thrashing from side to side of the enormous bed. Caught in some terrible nightmare, he was giving the heartrending moans that she had heard, clenching and unclenching his hands.

Still in the doorway, Jay froze. She felt a surge of compassion, a fierce longing to rush to him, and knew that she could not. She had no right to witness his very private disturbance, far less to reveal her knowledge of it; she must leave him alone.

Chapter Two

Jay woke to pale April sunlight after sleeping soundly for the remainder of the night. As soon as she'd returned to her own room the dreadful moans had ceased, and tired from her journey, exhaustion had proved stronger than concern for her host.

In daylight she found it hard to believe that she'd really gone to Rhys's room and found him so agitated, and she was thankful for the detachment lent by this feeling of unreality. This somber house was forbidding enough, without her increased misgivings about its owner.

Even the old-fashioned bathroom appeared more homey this morning. Jay enjoyed her bath, and then, having lingered longer than she'd intended, she dressed hurriedly and went to look for breakfast. Not sure where the meal would be served, she went to the room where they'd dined last evening. It was empty. She hesitated on the threshold, glancing around, and was enveloped in melancholy. The room must face west, because there was no welcome sunshine. Without the glowing candelabra everything looked inert, dead.

"Not in there, miss."

Preoccupied, Jay started when someone spoke just behind her. Trying to disguise her nervousness, she turned and met the speculative gray eyes of the woman who'd served dinner the night before.

"While Mrs. Godfrey is away, we have breakfast in the kitchen."

Jay was astonished. Rhys was the last person she would have expected to be so informal.

The kitchen seemed more modern than Jay anticipated, until she remembered Rhys's liking for gadgetry evident elsewhere.

"The house may be old, but Mr. Felstead doesn't believe in being out of date." The woman disconcerted Jay by seeming to read her thoughts.

Jay laughed awkwardly. "Did I make my surprise that obvious, Mrs. . . ." She paused. "I'm sorry. I don't think I was told your name."

"Harper, miss—Amy Harper. It wasn't that you looked surprised; I expect it, see. Not that the master has many visitors these days, but they all react the way you did. But I'm forgetting my manners—what do you fancy? Bacon perhaps and a couple of eggs?"

"Bacon would be lovely, thank you, but only one egg."

"You're nearly as bad as he is. Takes me all my time to get him to eat anything for breakfast. I don't like to see a man picking at his food."

"We ate very well last night," Jay began.

"Aye, I saw to that. But it was only because you were here," Mrs. Harper continued, her back to Jay as she trimmed the rind from bacon rashers.

"And where is Mr. Felstead now, has he gone out?"

"That I don't know. What I need to know, he tells me, and the rest is his business. More peaceful it is, that way. Mrs. Godfrey, now, she maintains as she has to know whether he's in or out, or where he'll be eating, but that doesn't go down at all well with the master."

"He seems to value his solitude."

"Don't you believe it, miss. That's only since—" She checked herself. "Aye, well, we'd best not go into that. But things might have been different."

"Did something go wrong?" Jay asked, thinking of the uneasy atmosphere.

"Wrong? It was terrible, Miss Stanmer, terrible. But we're forbidden to talk. Though nobody who'd seen what it did to Mr. Felstead could fail to sympathize, and it wasn't his fault, I swear it wasn't . . ."

"Fault?" Jay echoed, bewildered.

"I've done it again, haven't I? I can't keep a still tongue, even though I know he'll give me my walking papers if I breathe one word of it. He's sacked enough here because they've talked. Not that they said anything malicious, mind, but there are some things he won't have mentioned."

Mrs. Harper sighed as she turned bacon in the pan and popped bread into the toaster.

"I don't blame him; nothing can bring people back. It's best forgotten."

Mrs. Harper set Jay's plate before her and glanced toward the clock.

"You will excuse me now, won't you? I haven't begun on the bedrooms."

Alone, Jay found her thoughts turning inevitably to the snatches of tantalizing information. If some disturbing incident had occurred here, Rhys's tormented night was more explicable. She couldn't deny her curiosity about what had happened and why it affected him so.

She was still wondering about the sinister ambience of the house and its owner when the door behind her was thrust open and he walked in.

"Oh—good morning." He sounded surprised. "Where's Mrs. Harper?"

"Attending to the bedrooms, I believe."

"She would be. Never is around when I need her."

"It is a large house, and with your housekeeper away—"

"Don't reprove me again," he interrupted, then laughed dryly. "If I'm so hard on everyone, be thankful you're not going to be here very long."

He was looking intently at something he was holding in cupped hands. Jay wasn't sorry he was preoccupied, and that he seemed totally unaware that his moaning had woken her that night. She was beginning to relax when he spoke again, rather impatiently.

"Can't you give a hand then, since she isn't around?"

"Of course, if there's something I can do." She turned right around on her stool and faced him. "What . . . ?"

He nodded toward low cupboards. "See if you can locate a small box, will you? We'll have to improvise. I know—crumple some paper towels."

Jay hurried across to see what he was holding so gingerly. Gently, she laughed. "I didn't realize this was a rescue mission."

A tiny bird, desperately thin beneath ragged brown feathers, rested with one wing sticking out awkwardly, its head sagging against Rhys's thumb. Following his directions, she found a suitable box and then some paper towels, which she hastily crumpled.

"Good. Now, steady the box while I transfer him."

With infinite care, he lowered the injured creature

into its makeshift nest. Briefly, his hand rested on her
own. She was surprised by the gentleness of his touch
and somewhat disconcerted by the tremor that raced up
her arm.

"He was lucky I found him, trapped where we store
garden equipment. In this weather it wouldn't be used
for days. I don't know how we'll feed him."

"Warm milk?"

He glanced at her and grinned. "Why not?"

He wasn't wearing his spectacles. Jay thought he
looked years younger, and not nearly so chillingly
self-contained.

"Well, don't just stand staring," he said. "Find a
pan, will you?"

"It's *your* kitchen. You can't have less idea where
things are kept!"

He laughed again. "You always have an answer,
haven't you? All right, I'll find the pan. Just keep an
eye on our charge." After he'd put milk on to warm, he
looked toward her again. "I trust you've finished
breakfast?"

"More or less."

He nodded, glancing again toward the milk. "I'm not
certain what we'll use. Weren't fountain pen sacs the
thing for feeding small birds?"

"I don't know. We didn't rescue many in our New
York apartment."

She felt his sharp gaze. "You don't sound very
American."

"My father is, but I've lived in England for years
now."

He shrugged. "Anyway, I'm sure that's what I used
more than once when I was a child—centuries ago!"

Jay gave him a curious look. He seemed remarkably
more approachable. If he'd been this affable yesterday,
she might have begun her visit liking him.

He removed the pan from the stove, then searched purposefully through the cupboards for a package of drinking straws. "Can't think of anything else."

Jay watched, fascinated, while her host patiently drew up milk into the straw, then released it, drop by drop, into the yawning beak. She smiled, wondering again at the change in him, wishing ridiculously that something could erase all irascibility and nightmares and leave him like this, absorbed in a simple task, mellowed by it.

"Mrs. Harper can take this over," he remarked ruefully, "until Mrs. Godfrey returns and gives her instructions. I haven't the necessary patience."

Jay sensed though that he was enjoying the task as much as she liked watching him. Suddenly, however, he noticed her interest.

"I thought you were eager to see the paintings by daylight."

"I am, only . . ." She flushed, feeling embarrassed because he'd changed again and now resented her being there. Before he could say any more, Jay left. She went to her room and collected her notebook, pens, pencils, and her other tools. She would shut herself in that wretched room and keep out of Rhys's way for the rest of the day.

Drawing back the curtains made the room housing the pictures no more agreeable. Jay sighed. The early sun had disappeared and, in any case, the windows faced away from the morning light, making the corners beyond the four-poster bed gloomy. The feeling of misery persisted. It seemed silly to believe that a room or a house could have this appalling atmosphere, yet it appeared especially intense in here. She could easily believe Mrs. Harper's hints of some tragic occurrence, but why did it linger so?

*   *   *

"Don't you eat luncheon?"

Jay started again and cursed the apparent nervousness that made her jump when anyone here spoke to her. But it had grown dark, and busy with her work, she'd noticed no one approaching.

Rhys Felstead was regarding her solemnly from the doorway. Absurdly, he seemed no more eager than she to come into the room.

"I . . . er, wasn't feeling particularly hungry."

"I'm not surprised; it's a dreary room," he admitted, astonishing her, as he entered.

"Does it have a history?"

"My great-grandfather brought his French bride, Eugenie, to Scree Carr, just before their wedding. She's reputed to have slept in here, and was found dead on the terrace below."

"How tragic! How long had they been married when—"

"They hadn't," he interrupted brusquely. "It was their wedding day."

"Poor man. He must have suffered."

"He certainly didn't deserve that. By all accounts he was no saint and would have no regrets about her substantial dowry—at that time the Felsteads were anything but wealthy—but from his portrait he seemed to be a personable man. And he eventually became an eminent lawyer, so it seems he wasn't stupid either."

"Then why did she . . . I mean, *was* it suicide?"

"Evidently, Eugenie learned that he needed her money, and she couldn't be convinced that he loved her more than he loved her fortune."

"So that's why it feels so gloomy in here."

"Yes."

Rhys was still frowning, staring unseeingly toward the boarded windows. Jay sensed that there was more than some bygone Felstead bride behind his loathing of this place. She experienced a strong compulsion to reach out and grasp his arm, then suddenly his mood changed and he smiled.

"But you shouldn't let it put you off your food. The good Mrs. Harper won't approve. She's prepared another delicious soup, and in Mrs. Godfrey's absence she considers herself an expert in home-baked bread."

Turning from the pictures, Jay smiled. "Now you *are* tempting me!"

"If only with the food," he murmured, and turned away. He was running down the stairs before she'd recovered from the shock of his remark, delivered in a manner that, elsewhere, she'd have construed as provocative.

Jay quickly tidied her hair, washed her hands, and went downstairs.

"In here." Rhys called as she neared the dining room.

When she took the seat next to his, she sensed he was subdued.

"How goes it then?" he inquired, trying to sound casual. "Have you proved or disproved Paul Valentine's suspicions?"

"It's too early to talk about proof," Jay said carefully. "But I'm afraid I'm pretty certain that several of the paintings are copies."

"Before you go any further, Miss Stanmer, you'd better understand that if your verdict denies their authenticity, I'll seek a second opinion."

"You are, of course, at liberty to consult as many experts as you wish, but I don't lightly give a condemnation, and I will support my findings."

"Even so," he said coldly, "that is what I intend."

Jay wondered how Paul would react. By disputing

her opinion, Rhys could destroy Paul's faith in her ability to cope with the American job.

"Were all these paintings from the same source?" she asked.

"They were, but it has no relevance, so I don't plan to disclose it."

"But people with a collection of your caliber buy only through reputable channels."

"Quite."

"You could probably get back some of your investment if you revealed this."

"Miss Stanmer, I do not wish to pursue this aspect."

"If you say so."

Before the ensuing silence could become more awkward, they were interrupted by Mrs. Harper knocking, then hastily coming in.

"Oh, Mr. Felstead," she began agitatedly, "whatever am I going to do? My daughter's just telephoned; it's my husband, he's had an accident! It's snowing harder in the village, and he fell getting out of the van."

"I'm so sorry."

Mrs. Harper seemed close to tears. "Peggy, my daughter, would have gone with him, only she's got to look after the boy and . . . oh, what are we going to do? I can't leave you alone here with Mrs. Godfrey away—"

"Of course you can." Rhys rose immediately, went to Mrs. Harper, and grasped her shoulder. Jay felt her gaze drawn to his long fingers, which seemed to be willing the woman to accept his assurance.

"Mrs. Harper, you will go at once, and you won't give us another thought. Your husband needs you. That must be your only consideration."

"Oh, Mr. Felstead, that is a relief! I didn't know where to turn."

Jay noticed the difference in the woman's tone, and found herself still staring at Rhys' hand and wishing irrationally that she could experience a little of the comfort that seemed implicit in his touch.

"Anyone would suppose I'm totally incompetent," Rhys exclaimed to Jay, returning to the table. "And after all, if worst came to worst you could always condescend to assist with preparing meals."

She glanced at him and detected amusement behind the lenses.

"I take it you would cooperate, if the alternative were not eating?"

Jay grinned. "That—or leave," she said quickly.

"Is that what you think?" he murmured, but something in his manner implied that she would not readily be released.

As they finished their meal the outer door closed behind Mrs. Harper.

"How will she get home?" Jay asked. "Is the village very far?"

"A couple of miles, but it's fortunate that she's going now. Mrs. Harper bicycles here and with all this snow that can't be easy."

"Snow?" Recalling what the woman had said, Jay glanced out and was astonished to see flurries of flakes descending from a leaden sky.

"It has snowed all morning," Rhys exclaimed mockingly. "What have you been thinking about?"

First of all, Jay supposed, she'd been amazed by his rescue of the tiny bird, then perturbed to be banished as soon as she'd glimpsed his more agreeable side. After that, well, when she worked, it was always to the exclusion of everything else, and the upstairs room was so dark that she'd hardly noticed heavy skies. She was alternately annoyed and warmed by Rhys, but because of some hypnotic quality, she couldn't ignore him.

"Don't say you're too fascinated to think beyond these walls!"

She met the impact of his dark eyes head-on. By some uncanny means he'd learned her reactions—or surmised enough to be disconcerting.

"I see," he said when she didn't respond. "You were so occupied with work that you didn't notice anything else." His bland tone was mocking.

Jay rose hastily and returned to the disused bedroom where, though she might not like the atmosphere, she was at least free to think her own thoughts.

By late afternoon Jay was sure that further examination would only confirm that the paintings were faked. She'd gathered enough evidence to satisfy herself and Paul. She ought to be glad she'd finished. Tomorrow she would start for home—an agreeable solution. With no outside help in such a vast house, Rhys could hardly be pleased to have a guest.

When she told him over dinner that she intended leaving next morning his expression changed rapidly from consternation to wry amusement.

"Far be it from me to attempt to prolong your stay, Miss Stanmer, but you may find departing rather difficult. Mrs. Harper telephoned because, although she could leave her husband now, she can't get out of the village."

"We can't be snowbound at *Easter!*"

"How well do you know the Yorkshire moors, Miss Stanmer?"

She sighed. "Not very well."

"Ah." He seemed delighted by her alarm. "For the present you'll have to take my word. In daylight you may check to see whether the roads are impassable."

"Perhaps there'll be an overnight thaw . . ."

"Perhaps."

The night did not oblige; rather than a thaw it

brought keen winds which hurled the snow into drifts against the house and rattled the windows. Jay's only consolation was the absence of moans from Rhys's room, but during the long hours of darkness she was again conscious of the strange noise that resembled rushing water.

"How far are we from the coast?" she asked Rhys over breakfast the next day.

"Twenty miles or more as the crow flies, farther by road. You're surely not contemplating a visit?"

"No, when I leave I'll head straight for London. But I heard water—"

"You were mistaken."

"Has the bird survived?" Jay inquired, looking around for the box.

"Yes." He didn't smile.

"Have you fed him yet today?"

"Naturally. Even before I made something for you."

"If you want me to help in the kitchen, say so. I'd prefer that to veiled references to my being a nuisance."

Astonishing her again, Rhys laughed. "The references will be only thinly veiled, Miss Stanmer. And a bit of help would be welcome. You can begin by clearing away these things afterward."

She grinned at him. "That's better. I know you men don't like washing dishes."

"You've a vast experience of living with *us*, have you?"

Jay didn't wish to reply, but he rose and grasped her shoulder, as yesterday he had Amy Harper's, though his touch was anything but comforting.

"Well . . . ?"

"I've never lived with a man." Jay wondered why she'd told him.

"In that case, we must each make allowance for the

other in an unfamiliar situation," he murmured, his breath disturbing her hair.

Jay knew he was deliberately making her aware of her femininity; and she knew it was easy for him to do. She couldn't deny her attraction to him.

"I must get on." She stood abruptly, making him withdraw his hand.

"I thought your task on my paintings was completed?"

"If I'm compelled to remain, I may as well make more detailed notes."

The notes, however, took only until lunchtime. Snow had continued to fall through the night and intermittently since dawn, indicating even to Jay's inexperienced gaze that the roads beyond Scree Carr would be impassable.

After luncheon—omelets, which she'd admitted were delicious—she asked if Rhys required help preparing dinner. He thanked her, but informed her that Mrs. Godfrey kept the freezer well stocked and that it would feed them for days.

"Days? You said 'us'—I really can't stay here that long."

"You brought skis, did you?" he inquired, smiling. "Or a snowplow? A Range Rover maybe? That might get through in these conditions."

Jay didn't rise to his bait, but she didn't intend remaining caged indoors. "I'm going for a walk. I've had no fresh air since I arrived."

"I'd have thought there was sufficient permeating this house! But if you wish to walk, by all means . . . I'll come with you."

"No, I . . . no, thank you."

She needed to get away from this man who at the same time seemed coolly detached yet threatened to smother her. If she'd made a habit of admitting fear, she'd have acknowledged the alarm that Rhys generated in her.

The wind was bitterly cold but the snow had ceased and lay crisp under foot. It was so deep in places that it reached above her high boots. Jay set out, walking as briskly as she could. She heard the rushing water that she'd heard before and, eager to satisfy her curiosity, trudged toward the sound. With the snow whitening out all contours, it was difficult to discern anything in the landscape ahead that gave any clue to what produced the noise.

She walked to the rear of Scree Carr, where its windows were boarded over; it was more depressing in daylight than at night. Remembering Rhys's refusal to explain, she shivered, and, keeping her head down, continued toward the puzzling sound of water.

The snow began again suddenly, driven into her back by the strong wind. Jay turned up her collar, holding it to her ears, and struggled on.

"Not that way." He made her jump as, soft-footed in the snow, he overtook her and barred her way. In the sheepskin jacket, Rhys seemed as implacable as a giant oak. He turned her around, his grip viselike on her arm, but when he kept his fingers locked on her, Jay wasn't sorry. Turned into the wind, she caught the snow full blast, beating into her eyes and mouth. Although she blinked, snowflakes made her eyes water.

"What is it?" Rhys asked, his tone altered, concerned.

"Nothing, I . . . seem to have got an eye full of snow."

"Let me see."

He made her face him, blocking the wind, and she tried again to blink away the snow and look at him but her eyes misted.

"It's like stars on your lashes," he murmured, his voice strange.

"I'm fine now," Jay said quickly as her vision cleared. "I can see perfectly again." She could see *him*, his eyes very dark and bright without the glasses, gazing intently into her own.

She moistened her lips.

He'd been steadying her with a hand on each shoulder; suddenly they slid around her back. She felt their warmth through the fur of her coat.

"Jay," Rhys whispered. His lips came down on hers, almost brutally at first, but then she felt a subtle change, as his mouth moved, willing her to respond. When his tongue tentatively traced her lips, they parted.

Jay leaned into him, oblivious of the blizzard continuing about them, oblivious to everything except Rhys holding her close, and the pulsing warmth that penetrated through the thickness of their coats.

When at last his lips released hers, Rhys looked deep into her eyes. He removed one of her gloves and pressed her fingers to his lips, his eyes still conjuring spirals of delight right through her. When they walked on, he held her hand and carried it into his pocket.

"Can you run?" Rhys asked, over the buffeting wind.

"I can try." His kiss had left her breathless and uncertain of anything.

He squeezed her fingers. "This way then."

Approaching the house, he glanced toward the boarded windows. Jay felt his sigh, and her hand tightened on his.

"Any breath left?" he asked, looking toward her.

"Not very much," Jay admitted and they slowed to a brisk walk.

She noticed a door. "Can't we go in that way?"

"That door's never used."

They entered the kitchen and stamped snow from their boots on the mat.

"I'm afraid the weather is no more hospitable than your host!"

Jay grinned up at him. "I'm learning to adjust."

"To which?" Rhys asked, raising a dark eyebrow.

"Perhaps to both."

He laughed, seeming very much younger. An icy trickle slithered down the side of his face, which he dashed away without glancing from her.

"You're drenched, Jay, you mustn't catch cold. Would you like a hot drink?"

"Later, perhaps, when I've taken off these wet things."

He nodded. "A hot bath wouldn't hurt either of us. Give me your coat."

He took the bedraggled fur as she eased out her arms, but he remained motionless afterward, his dark eyes still seeking hers.

"Your hair is soaked," he said, and she felt the back of his fingers, a caress above her ear.

"It's not the first time it's been wet, you know," she said lightly, not wanting to go anywhere while his eyes were holding her to him.

Again, Rhys smiled. "Your cheeks are glowing, anyway." His hand strayed from her hair to her cheek. "But how cold you are!" he exclaimed, his smile dying. "I mustn't keep you from your bath."

Since Rhys had caught up with her outdoors, Jay had experienced a dizzying excitement, and it lasted while she bathed and dried her hair.

How different Rhys was today, and how unsettling, she thought. The kiss had astonished her, yet when his lips claimed her own she had known it had been prophesied, more than once, in the expression in those dark eyes. What astonished her more was her own response. It wasn't like the composed Jay Stanmer to stand out in a blizzard exchanging kiss for kiss with any man, much less a man she hardly knew.

But did she hardly know him? Wasn't Rhys revealing far more than she'd expected of his true self? After his cold reception, there had been occasions when she'd glimpsed a very different person . . . a man strong enough to permit himself to show concern—for an injured bird, for Amy Harper, and now for Jay herself.

The hot water had relaxed her, and now, brushing her hair, Jay realized she felt desperately sleepy. Hugging her robe about her, she crossed to the bed. But for the firelight, the room was nearly dark. Beyond the windows snow was still falling steadily, from a sky almost as black as night.

She must have dropped off at once, and deeply; jolted awake, she felt the sense of unreality that follows daytime sleep. Looking at her watch, trying to reorient herself, Jay heard moaning and knew it had wakened her.

For several long minutes she lay there listening, tense, aware that she couldn't bear it. When it intensified, she rose swiftly, thrust her feet into fur slippers, and crossed the landing.

Wearing a robe, lying on the top of the covers, Rhys was asleep, his face painfully contorted. His hands were clenched so tightly that the knuckles had whitened.

Jay crossed to the bed and stood, frowning, at the foot.

Clearly, he was dreaming. A groan was dragged from him. Instinctively, she came around the bed to his side, and when he thrust out a fist, she took it in both hands. Sitting on the bed, Jay willed him to calm.

"Don't," she whispered, "Rhys, don't . . ."

His lips parted, this time to form a silent word, and although he flung his head from side to side, the moaning didn't immediately recur. Just as Jay was beginning to believe the dream had passed, though, his fingers gripped hers fiercely, threatening to snap her bones.

"God, no!" he gasped, eyes still closed, his hand jerking free.

"It's all right, Rhys," Jay said softly, and grasped his shoulder, trying to reach him in the nightmare.

He turned slightly, and strained toward her, then suddenly his eyes opened. "Get out, Jay." He tried to move away.

"No." Their kiss out in the snow had aroused more than sensuality. She didn't understand all her emotions, but leaving would deny them.

"Let me alone."

Smiling sadly, she shook her head. "This isn't the first time, is it?"

He scowled. "Have you been in here before?"

"Only as far as the door. Anyone can have nightmares."

"In the middle of the day?" he asked bitterly.

Her fingers tightened over his shoulder, and she gazed into his eyes.

"You don't know what you're doing, Jay, you should leave."

"Give me one good reason."

"You don't know me. I'm hardly responsible when I'm like this."

"If you mean you're not quite so icily contained, is that so bad?"

He snorted ruefully. "One must exercise some control; otherwise . . ."

". . . a few emotions might show through? Is that what you're saying?"

"And more. Jay you know what happened out there."

She smiled. "Do I appear so very naive? Rhys, except for me, you're alone in this great house. I can't just walk away."

"You'll learn nothing," he said sharply.

"So, all right, I don't mean to pry. For heaven's sake, relax."

A log shifted in the fireplace, sending out a flurry of sparks and the scent of wood smoke. He stared toward it, seeming to withdraw. Beyond the windows the blizzard continued, hurling snowflakes against the glass and sighing, like some restless spirit, through boughs that scratched the panes. Jay shivered. Rhys started and smiled wryly.

"You see, you're cold. You should have gone."

"To my own room? Or away from here?"

"One or the other."

"No." She knew she couldn't. It didn't make any kind of sense, but she felt held to this man by some invisible bond that was unbreakable.

His laugh was dry, little more than a snort. "Relax, you said. You don't know what you're asking. However . . ." He stretched out more comfortably then, slipped an arm about her, and drew her nearer until her head rested on his shoulder. She felt his lips on her hair.

"You hear the storm, Jay. Don't you see there's just as much danger here?"

"You won't alarm me. This isn't like the room where the pictures are."

"Oh . . . there." She felt tension spreading through his body.

"There's more to that room than some suicidal Felstead bride, isn't there?"

"You said you wouldn't pry," he reminded her sharply, drawing away.

"I'm sorry," Jay said stiffly. "I'm accustomed to showing just a little concern for people I know; I can't discipline it all the time."

"Jay," Rhys said, his voice somber. "I can't let you care. You're here to do a job; that has to be all."

When she looked into his eyes, she realized that all the time he was saying the words he was thinking, hoping, something quite different. She bit back the snarl rising to her lips and smiled instead.

"Don't mix business with pleasure?"

"I wish it were that simple."

Again, she felt his lips on her hair, then brushing her cheek, but when she glanced up his eyes were still troubled. She smiled again, willing him to let go.

Rhys sighed. "I did try to make you leave," he said huskily, before his hard mouth sought hers.

Jay responded instantly, her lips stirring under his, then parting so his tongue tasted hers. Tiny darts of excitement tingled through her every pore, making each nerve ending vibrantly alive, making her cling to him.

"Why, Jay, why?" he asked against her throat. "Why do I want you so much? You've been here, what—two days? Why this?"

"Is it so unpredictable?" She needed him so much, so inexplicably—so completely!

"You're saying this is merely sexual attraction?"

"I don't know."

But she did know that if the deep and very real urge to get closer to him had been limited to desire, she wouldn't have remained in the room so readily.

Rhys kissed her again, urgently, and his arms tightened, crushing her to him. His fingers traced her spine, sending quivers of tantalizing delight spiraling through her to join the dizziness in her head. When Rhys surrendered her lips, Jay sought his mouth again, teasing with her tongue until his lips curved into a smile and he began nibbling sensuously at her mouth.

"Jay," he groaned. "You've got to get out of here. Don't you know what is happening?"

"I think I know you. You live a disciplined life."

He laughed, his dark eyes bright with delighted amusement. And then he kissed her again, more in affection than attraction.

"*Touché*. But don't stake too much on it. I've been alone for one hell of a long time."

"I know." Awareness of the reluctant solitude in which Rhys lived hurt her, as much as the understanding that he would still exclude her.

"Haven't you earned a little enjoyment?"

"Without price? There have always been two kinds of woman with me, Jay. The ones who'd accept that I could need them for that moment, without expecting any more, and . . ." He paused. "Oh, forget it," he said, sounding angry, and was silent.

"And the marrying kind?" Jay asked, smiling. "At least you're straightforward about there being a difference."

"And you know I wouldn't insult you by letting this get out of hand."

Torn between her longing to linger in his arms and mistrust of the heady excitement generated by having him near, Jay rose and crossed the carpet, but when she reached the door, Rhys was at her side.

"There is just one thing . . ." he said quietly.

Jay glanced up at him.

Gently, he grasped her arm, sending sparks escalating toward her shoulder. "Thanks, anyway—for coming."

He drew her to him, his arms locking around her as his hard body made contact with hers through their robes. Surprised by his unmistakable need, Jay failed to control a tiny gasp. Smiling, Rhys kissed her again, tenderly at first, but soon his tongue was exploring her lips again while his hands began stirring over her back.

"You see," he murmured breathlessly, as he hauled his mouth away from hers. "You'd better go."

When she reached her room, Jay noticed how short of breath she was, and smiled wryly. She'd always thought Rhys disturbing. She couldn't have guessed how easily he would make her dismiss every reservation about him.

Before dressing for dinner she sat for a long while, gazing into the fire, thinking. How had this happened? How—why—had she lowered all defenses with Rhys? What was so special about him that he'd gotten through to her where Paul Valentine had never succeeded? Paul, who was kind, attentive, all the things Rhys was unlikely to be. Paul, who had escorted her to romantic places, who was always ready to offer a sympathetic ear. What was there about Rhys to make her even imagine having him make love to her?

Chapter Three

"What do you do with your time?"

"Do?" Rhys raised a quizzical dark eyebrow. "Do you imagine the estate runs itself?"

Smiling, Jay shook her head. "You needn't sound so indignant; I'm not criticizing. But you must have people to help run the place."

"A farm manager, yes, a head gardener who has two or three men under him, the lodge keeper, whom you've seen, domestic staff."

"That wasn't quite what I meant. Don't you get bored?"

Rhys smiled to himself. "I don't spend my days wandering the house, admiring my collection of paintings, if that's what you think."

"I didn't." She was trying desperately to find things to talk about. As she might have guessed, after the interlude in his bedroom, neither of them were very relaxed, and she felt sorry. Although she couldn't regret any of their kisses, she'd have sacrificed them if it would have restored the sense of camaraderie that she and Rhys were beginning to feel for each other.

Dinner last evening had been difficult; throughout the meal she'd been acutely conscious of the brown eyes which constantly sought her face, and of the attraction leaping the short distance between them at the table. Rhys might prevent further physical contact, but no one on this earth could contain the force, fierce as electricity, surging between them.

And today, across the kitchen table, Rhys need only look—as he was looking now—to make her incapable of dragging away her gaze.

"When do you go to New York?" he asked coldly, and his glance swung away, to rest in apparent absorption on the coffee percolator.

"New York? I . . . didn't know I'd said . . ."

"*You* didn't, Paul Valentine did. He certainly believes your expertise will be an asset in America, if a loss to him in London."

"I see." Jay shrugged, reluctant now to think about the venture. "We haven't finalized any details yet."

"I thought you'd be eager; you said you're part American."

"My father's a New Yorker, but since my parents split up I've remained over here."

"Your mother's English, is she?"

"She was," Jay said quickly, and felt his gaze returning to her.

"Oh," Rhys said hastily, "I'm sorry. I didn't know."

"It was a year ago now, anyway."

"Who's to say how much time is enough for adjusting?" Rhys was tracing patterns with a spoon, too disturbed for mere concern on her behalf.

"Was your own loss recent?" she asked softly.

"Mine?" He was wary.

"Your parents. Surely they're not around?"

"Oh, that. No, they died years ago."

Jay didn't know what to say. She sensed he was recalling some still-raw bereavement, yet if he refused to confide, she couldn't help, however desperately she longed to try.

"Mrs. Harper rang to say the thaw has begun in the village," he announced abruptly. "You'll be able to leave. If not today, first thing tomorrow," he added fiercely, convincing her he was thankful.

Jay nodded, wishing she felt relieved.

"You haven't spelled it out, but I gather that examining the paintings has confirmed that they're not authentic?"

"I'm afraid so. Rhys, I'm sorry—"

"Your regret's a surprise, at least. Small comfort, however. You know I intend to obtain a second opinion."

As he rose to go he mentioned another painting he wished her to appraise, one he wouldn't sell.

"I'll show you later. Naturally, I'll pay your fee."

"There's no need, Rhys. I'm here, after all, with very little to do."

"And would Valentine approve? You shouldn't give away services, surely?"

"Paul doesn't own me."

Rhys smiled slightly but didn't comment. "I must be on my way."

"Anything I can do to help while you're out?"

He shook his head. "I should leave it all for Mrs. Harper. She'll expect to sort out the chaos. We'd better convince her she's needed."

"But I thought, with Mrs. Godfrey away as well . . ."

"Believe me, Mrs. Harper treasures Mrs. Godfrey's absences, don't deprive her!" He hesitated, glancing seriously toward her, as if weighing her reaction, yet his tone became casual.

"You wanted to know how I occupy my time; be ready in ten minutes. I'll show you where I'm going, then you can walk back through the estate."

Rhys's handling of the Rolls Royce over frozen snow was a delight. Jay was so busy admiring his skill in negotiating the sharp bends of the narrow road that she hardly noticed the route they were taking.

When he gradually slowed the car outside gates set in walls even higher than those surrounding his home, she looked up with a start.

"I shall be here for most of the day," he said quickly. "Enjoy your walk. You can see Scree Carr from here. You shouldn't lose your way."

As he drove off, Jay gazed after the Rolls, but the hand she'd raised in a cheery wave dropped to her side. Her gray eyes clouded as she saw two words on the sign beside the drive: PSYCHIATRIC HOSPITAL.

Slowly, she began walking through the park. So that was it. Rhys couldn't tell her, but he had to let her know he was receiving treatment.

"No," she murmured plaintively, "no." It wasn't that she felt there was any stigma attached to needing psychiatric help, nor was she afraid that he was in some way "different." It was simply that she didn't want to contemplate *him* undergoing anything so disturbing.

"There must be another way," she said, still aloud, then continued her reasoning silently. So Rhys suffered appalling nightmares, but he was just as rational as she was. He was lonely, too much alone, and had evidently suffered a bereavement that still affected him. But all he needed was a bit of affection . . . *love.*

Why am I thinking like this? Jay asked herself. Why do I care?

She was halfway to the house when she again heard

the strange sound of running water. This time, she was determined to explore.

Walking was slow over the snow-covered ground and treacherous in places where the snow had drifted, making it impossible to judge what lay beneath the white blanketing. It was half an hour before Jay reached the edge of the escarpment, and what she saw then was so utterly beautiful that she let out a long, wondering gasp.

The ground dropped away steeply, a narrow gorge sliced through the rock, with giant boulders thrusting through the snow on each side of the ravine. To her left, a waterfall, swollen by melting snow, plummeted about fifty feet into a swirling pool, dark as the surrounding rocks. From the pool the river hurtled over a series of lesser falls, then tore over its stony bed toward the far end of the chasm.

Jay stood motionless, absorbing the splendor of the scene, awed by its magnificence. Icicles which had formed on the adjacent rocks surrendered their hold on frosted stone to fall, tinkling into myriad glistening fragments, before the water swallowed them.

Above the roaring of the cascade she heard an eerie keening, half-familiar, and glimpsed, against a bare-limbed tree, a swooping sea gull. Remembering, she shivered. She could believe that this same bird had heralded her arrival at Scree Carr, yet why should she feel afraid now? What could threaten her? She'd met Rhys, had found him more human than she'd anticipated—so human that he needed assistance in learning to accept the unacceptable? What had occurred to disturb him? And why on earth did she feel so concerned . . .

"You shouldn't be here."

The reproof, from a few paces behind her, startled

Jay so that she nearly overbalanced and fell over the cliff. Furious, she swung round.

She wouldn't have been surprised to face Rhys's implacable stare; meeting a pair of blue eyes, level with her own, Jay felt disconcerted.

"Who are you?" she demanded, disliking the man immediately.

The lined face, tanned to the shade of a robin's wing, crinkled further, as a frown settled above inflexibly glaring eyes.

"I'd ask *you* that, miss, if I didn't know the master had a guest. But you're seeking trouble, by prying. If Mr. Felstead finds you here . . ."

"Mr. Felstead is out," she interrupted, angry and rather scared.

"Aye, you'd have been careful to make sure! But he's not the only one can warn you there's some places shouldn't be investigated."

"But this is a part of his estate. Mr. Felstead suggested I walk—"

"Walk, yes. Go poking your nose into what doesn't concern you, no."

"I don't have to listen to you," Jay said, pushing past, but though he was older, the man was strong; when he grabbed her wrist she couldn't free herself.

"We all have our troubles and expect strangers to respect our privacy."

"But I don't see—"

His laugh was harsh, as wild as the landscape. "You see enough. We don't like your sort, coming here, stirring up the past—"

"You can't know who I am, you must be mistaken," Jay protested. "Mr. Felstead invited me to examine some paintings, that's all."

"Aye. Aye, like I said—poking around."

He released her suddenly with a jerk, while Jay was struggling. She rubbed the tender spot where his fingers had chafed through her kid gloves.

"Is it tomorrow you're leaving?" he demanded, his blue eyes staring.

"I haven't yet decided, and that's hardly your business."

"I could make it mine. Since you're going, there may be no need."

Before she could question his manner, the man was running, surprisingly surefooted in the snow, toward the mansion. Jay wasn't at all sure what to make of him. His wizened face suggested he was quite old, yet his agility revealed that he might be younger than she'd supposed. But who was he? And why was he angry that she'd discovered the waterfall?

Approaching the house, Jay's glance was drawn again to the wood covering every rear window. Why had they been boarded over? And why did they make her feel overwhelmingly depressed?

As she walked toward the front entrance, she realized how perturbed she was feeling. First there'd been the upset of learning where Rhys was compelled to spend his day, then the alarming encounter with the old man, now this reminder of her interest in these windows being quashed—*by Rhys*.

Passing the kitchen, she jumped when someone tapped on the window, but was relieved when she saw Amy Harper once more at the sink.

"Come in this way, Miss Stanmer, it's a trudge round to the front."

Jay willingly complied. Rhys's daily woman was an agreeable body, blessedly ordinary, a rare asset in this household.

"You're no longer snowbound!" Jay exclaimed, stamping snow from her boots onto the mat.

"Can't say I'm sorry, miss. Not with my hubby laid up."

"How is he?"

"He'll live. Got his leg in plaster. Like me, he is, though, can't stand being idle. But how've you and Mr. Felstead been managing?"

Remembering what Rhys had said, Jay smiled. "We've coped, I think. But I'm sure we're both delighted to have you take charge again."

"I thought as much. Still, I was glad the master wasn't on his own. You never can tell with him, not how he'll be . . ." She shook her head, checked herself, and smiled at Jay. "But this won't do, me gossiping while you're standing there. Let me take your coat. Do you want some coffee? It's nearly eleven, and you look quite peaky."

By the time Mrs. Harper had made coffee, Jay was thawing out before the kitchen fire. Her thoughts were thawing also, reassured by the other woman's presence. She was still interested to know what was perturbing Rhys.

"Mrs. Harper," she began warily, sipping from the steaming cup, "I'm not just being nosey, but what is wrong here? There's such an overwhelming sadness about the place, and then there's Mr. Felstead himself. . . . He took me as far as the hospital gates. Why is he having treatment?"

"Treatment?" Mrs. Harper asked, something odd about her voice.

Jay sighed. "I've done it again, haven't I? Asked a question I shouldn't. Believe me, it's only that I care . . ."

Mrs. Harper was staring at her enigmatically. Suddenly she blinked, reached for a cup, and poured coffee for herself. Leaning against the draining board, she drank deeply and looked at Jay again.

"Is that right, do you care? About him, I mean?"

Jay gave a little laugh. "Well, why not? We both like the same things, paintings, antiques. He's an intelligent man."

"*And* attractive. Don't ask *me* then, love, ask *him.* Get him to tell you everything."

"I couldn't, he'd be embarrassed. He'd never confide."

"He might, he just might . . ." Mrs. Harper pensively sipped her coffee. "I'm sorry, miss, I'm going to tell you nothing, not one word. It has to come from him. He always has reasons for everything he does."

"Fair enough. But tell me, who is that old man I saw on the estate—I don't mean Manners at the lodge. He's about my height, with a face baked brown by the weather."

"Sharp blue eyes, and aggressive? That's Mike Travers, the gardener."

"He told me off for being near the waterfall. I couldn't think why—still can't."

"The waterfall? Oh, dear." Mrs. Harper had paled. "Whatever you do, don't let Mr. Felstead know that you've been there."

Jay swallowed back a flock of questions. "Very well. I suppose there's no chance you'll reveal why that would annoy him?"

"None, I'm afraid." Although firm, her voice was regretful.

"I was afraid of that too. All in all, we've a pretty mysterious household, haven't we?"

"It hasn't always been like this, you know. A few years back . . ."

"You've worked here a long time, have you?"

"I have that! Me and Mrs. Godfrey longer than any of the others. Travers has been here only since last July; Manners at the lodge since the winter before. And although Travers has help in the gardens, in summer they live out, away from the estate. When we need extra help indoors, Mrs. Godfrey brings in one or two of her nieces."

Long before she set down her empty cup, Jay understood she would learn nothing from Amy Harper. As she went up to her room she felt heavyhearted, not nearly so cheerful as she'd expected to feel about leaving.

During the afternoon, Jay interrupted the packing she'd begun to take a final look at the paintings that had brought her to Scree Carr.

The sun that had aided the thaw was brightening the forbidding room. When she'd reexamined the pictures, she glanced again at her notes, then was tempted to linger. Encouraged by the additional light, she drew back the curtains from the windows that were boarded over, and stared hard, frowning, willing them to yield their secret.

The door creaked open and she started, afraid.

"Like a cup of tea, Miss Stanmer?"

Jay nodded. "Thanks." She was thankful it was only Amy Harper. Taking the cup, she noticed that Amy was looking toward the windows. "Is this yet another secret?"

Mrs. Harper sighed. "Poor Mr. Felstead—cruel it was. No wonder he couldn't face being reminded. Don't ask him, will you, Miss Stanmer?"

"Very well." Jay went to pull the curtains across.

Mrs. Harper glanced toward the paintings. "Have you finished in here?"

"I think so."

"Then come on down. A gloomy place this is, and no mistake. Don't you become obsessed with it, like she did . . ."

"She?"

The little woman clamped her lips together, shaking her head. "The master'll be home any second."

Mrs. Harper went on ahead. Alone, Jay hurried down the staircase, feeling utterly dejected. She'd been on the brink of learning what really was so disturbing about that room, yet suddenly she wasn't certain that she wanted to know. It might be too upsetting.

Deep in thought, she didn't notice footsteps behind her on the stairs. When someone pushed past her, she jumped yet again, annoyed at her shredding nerves. It was Mike Travers.

"One moment please," she called after him.

He hesitated, then turned his head. "Yes?" he snapped.

"I didn't realize who you were this morning. I'm sorry if I appeared to question your right to query my presence."

"It was for your own good. You don't know Mr. Felstead like we do. If he found you by the waterfall, there's no knowing what he'd do."

"Now, just a minute," she began.

At that moment the front door opened. Rhys came striding into the hall.

"Jay!" he exclaimed, smiling. Their eyes met and held, and an ecstatic quiver ran through her spine. He couldn't have seemed more assured.

Unnoticed, the old man left her. Rhys stopped him and murmured, "Have you fixed it?" then nodded. Travers hurried to the door. Smiling again, Rhys ran up the stairs to join her. He seized her hand. "Let's take a look at that painting I mentioned."

He was still holding her hand when they reached the attic. Jay's awareness of him intensified, a heady delight preventing her taking in all that he was saying as he opened a door at the head of narrow stairs.

He glanced sideways at her, raising an eyebrow.

"Where's the composed art expert who arrived here? Aren't you pleased at the opportunity to examine a Degas?"

"If it's genuine, I'll be thrilled. Don't blame me for being cautious."

"Ah." Rhys's smile was wry. He removed the spectacles and scrutinized her face, which Jay knew had flushed. "Cautious, or preoccupied?"

Before releasing her hand, his fingers tightened over hers.

Jay swallowed, trying to control the tingle of excitement, and the steady pulsing that was increasing deep within her.

"Is this the picture you mean?" she asked briskly, crossing quickly to a painting that had been leaned against a chest of drawers.

"That's the one."

While she gazed at the picture, Rhys came to her. His hand rested on her shoulder, only lightly, but his fingers were burning through her dress. He stepped even closer and she felt the heat from his body at her back, bridging the space between them.

When she remained motionless, his fingers tightened on her shoulder, conveying wordless approval; she couldn't imagine why that pleased her. She'd always hated men who took advantage of any pretext for contact.

His sudden laugh, though gentle, made her start. "I'll leave you undisturbed," he said, and hurried out.

Jay went down on one knee on the rug in front of the picture. Already she knew instinctively that this was a genuine Degas, but she couldn't afford to be wrong. She examined the painting, inch by inch, for telltale strokes that might have indicated it was forged. Kneeling on both knees, she bent her head to check the signature.

As she moved, the floor gave beneath her weight. Timber cracked ominously. Unable to save herself, Jay plunged down. There was no time to feel more than momentary terror; she'd crashed to the floor of the room below before she really believed she was falling.

Cautiously, Jay tested first one leg, then the other. They had crumpled beneath her, but although her entire body was shaken and bruised, no bones seemed to be broken.

For a few seconds she rested, gazing disbelievingly around at the plaster and splintered wood that had fallen with her, and then up toward the gap in the ceiling. When she was breathing more steadily, she slowly got to her feet. She felt quite dizzy and the back of her head was sore; rubbing the spot she'd hit, she staggered to the door.

It opened before she got there and Rhys looked anxiously into the room. "Jay? What the hell—" He saw the hole in the ceiling and the debris beneath. "Oh, my God!"

He reached her in a stride or so and put his arm round her. "Are you all right?"

"I . . . think so." She felt reassured already, much better.

"We'll make certain." He found her a chair, then hurried to the telephone and dialed. "I'm calling Dr. Milner."

Rhys wouldn't accept that sending for the doctor was unnecessary. After checking that she could walk, he took her to her room and remained there till Dr. Milner arrived.

Rhys seemed as shocked as Jay herself. After asking what had happened, he sank into worried silence, broken only by his repeated inquiries about whether she felt at all better.

As soon as Jay saw Dr. Milner, a large, comfortable

man in a thick sweater and tweeds, she relaxed, confident he'd soon assure her.

"I don't believe I'm seriously hurt," she told him.

She was faced by smiling hazel eyes. "We'll soon see, won't we?" He glanced toward Rhys. "Give us five minutes or so."

When Rhys had left, Dr. Milner assisted Jay from the chair to the bed.

"You're certainly walking too well for anyone with fractured bones. But we'll check you over thoroughly, just the same. How did the accident happen? Rhys said something about a trap door giving way."

"So that's what it was. I couldn't think how the floor collapsed."

The doctor smiled. "It'd all have been over before you realized."

"That's right. One minute I was examining the painting, the next . . ." She smiled ruefully. "There isn't any real damage, though, is there?"

Dr. Milner tested every limb, then began pressing various parts of her body. "Have you any internal pain of any kind?"

"None."

"Are you certain now?"

"Positive. I just feel a bit battered. Otherwise I'm fine."

"You'll certainly be sore for a while—I'm afraid you'll find new bruises every time you move—but there seems to be no real damage."

Dr. Milner was completing his examination when Rhys knocked. "Well?" he asked, worriedly, as he entered.

"You were wise to call me in, Rhys, but I'm pretty confident your guest has suffered no more than bruising and a thorough shaking."

"Thank heavens!"

"You ought to keep your home in better repair. I thought you did. I'm surprised at you, neglecting the place so much that it begins to collapse."

"You know me better than that, Henry. Whatever else, I'm not guilty of neglect. I simply don't understand. That trap door is never used."

"Well, you don't need me to tell you how serious this might have been. I dare say you'll get it attended to at once." The doctor glanced at his watch and then turned to Jay. "I'll leave you these tablets, a simple pain killer, in case you don't rest too well tonight."

He asked then if it had been Rhys's day at the hospital.

"Yes, and I'll be there again tomorrow."

"Good, good. You know how vital that is."

After the doctor had left, Rhys insisted that Jay rest. He seemed reluctant to leave her bedside, and drew up a chair.

"How can I begin to apologize?" he said solemnly, the dark eyes behind the lenses revealing his deep concern.

"You couldn't have predicted the accident. I'm not blaming you."

"I'm still sorry." He paused for a second, pensively. "Did you have a chance to form any opinion on that painting?"

"Naturally, proof would take time. But I'm certain it's genuine."

His smile was rueful. "That makes it seem worse." Removing his glasses, he stared down at them, avoiding her eyes.

"I'm afraid I was testing you. I bought that picture through Christie's. They'd satisfied me about its authenticity."

"But you doubted me. You wondered if I'd only

claimed the others were faked because the idea had been sown in my mind?"

"It was unforgivable, I know."

Jay smiled. "Unduly cautious maybe. But you don't know me, do you?"

"Not professionally, not yet."

"And those seven paintings matter to you."

He frowned and his eyes veiled. "There's a lot of money involved," he said quickly, and Jay knew there was more than their value at stake.

"Time's running out; now the snow's going, I'll be leaving tomorrow."

His gaze jerked toward her face again. "Does Henry say you're fit?"

"He hasn't said I'm not."

"Wouldn't remaining here another day be wiser?"

"I don't believe that's at all necessary."

"I see." Rhys sounded cross. He thrust the spectacles back onto his nose, then hurried to the door.

Joining him for dinner, Jay was disturbed. He appeared completely withdrawn, answering in monosyllables when addressed, and making no attempt to fill the silence when she herself wasn't speaking.

How strange Rhys was! It seemed incredible that he'd held her close, out there in the snowstorm, and later in his room. Recalling the intimacy of their embrace, and the yearning it had generated, her cheeks flared.

Hating the awkwardness, Jay excused herself immediately after dinner. She packed everything but her overnight things, took a bath, then got into bed. As an afterthought, she reached for Dr. Milner's tablets. She had a long drive ahead tomorrow. Neither her own aches and pains, nor any possible disturbance from across the landing, should prevent sleep.

When Jay woke, it was fully daylight. Horrified, she saw that the time was nine o'clock. She'd intended an early start.

She found Amy Harper alone in the kitchen.

"You've had a good sleep, Miss Stanmer, haven't you? The master said to let you rest."

"Is he around?" Jay asked, although she'd sensed he wasn't.

"Lord, no, miss. He was off early, just driving away as I arrived."

"I see." She was disappointed she wouldn't see him again. "No matter. I'll be in touch with him about the pictures."

"He said I was to tell you he feels you ought to stay on another day."

Jay wavered. Didn't she want to see him again? But she remembered last evening's uneasy meal and knew she couldn't take another. She didn't wish to analyze the reason, but when Rhys withdrew it stung.

"No, I'm all right, really; I'd better go."

When she returned to her room, her head was throbbing dully and the back of her skull was still tender to the touch. She sighed wryly; she would indeed be sore for some time yet. Still puzzled about the accident, she left her bedroom and went up to the room into which she'd fallen.

No one had removed the debris, but then Rhys was unlikely to clear up the rubble, and Mrs. Harper would have left for home after dinner last night.

Kneeling, Jay began sifting fragments of wood and plaster, wondering how the trap door had collapsed. Running her fingers through the dust, she found a scattering of glittering particles. They looked like brass; swiftly, she examined the trap door. Its hinges were brass . . . and each was snapped along a line clearly made by a saw.

As panic tightened her throat, Jay inspected the hinges again, then sprang up. With just one backward glance, she sped from the room.

In her bedroom she flung the remaining items into her case, snatched up her coat, and ran down the stairs. In the hall she hesitated, wanting to say good-bye to Amy, yet not daring to risk anything that might impede her departure. In five minutes she was driving rapidly away from Scree Carr.

She'd wondered and wondered about Rhys ever since her arrival. Now the pieces were fitting together and the picture they formed was grotesque. Rhys was enigmatic, a man of mercurial moods. He was also powerful, unaccustomed to being crossed. Obsessive about those seven paintings, wasn't he capable of going to any lengths to prevent someone revealing they were faked?

Chapter Four

"You can't claim I didn't warn you."

"I know, Paul." Jay sighed. Avoiding his amused green eyes, her gaze slid past him to the exclusive gown displayed in the window across the street from the gallery.

"Because Felstead's such a brooding individual doesn't mean that you've got to remain infected. You've scarcely smiled during the fortnight since you returned."

"You're exaggerating again, I haven't been that bad. It's just that Rhys appears so isolated, and I can't help wondering why."

Paul snorted. "Oh, come on, Jay. Who'd want to live with *that?*"

She swallowed back her instinctive argument. She couldn't recall how Rhys had come into their conversation, but he had, as he had repeatedly since her return.

"Forget him, Jay," Paul advised sharply.

She glanced toward him, smiling ruefully. She knew Paul's advice wasn't without a tinge of jealousy and she resolved to try to control what was becoming an obsession with Rhys Felstead. She turned to open the pack of catalogs just delivered by the printers.

"We can't dismiss him entirely when he's seeking a second opinion," she added reasonably.

"He's paid for our time, hasn't he? And as for consulting someone else, we've had that out, haven't we?"

They certainly had. Paul had been furious that Rhys wasn't satisfied with her verdict. She ought to be thankful he let the subject rest while they attended to other business.

Paul looked quickly at his watch. "Time I was off. I've another appointment after I've seen our account- ants. But I'll look in here on my way home." He smiled engagingly. "Doing anything tonight?"

"Nothing special—why?"

"We must discuss the American gallery. Much as I'll hate losing you, I need someone reliable out there, Jay. We'll go round to my place, have a bite to eat, and finalize arrangements."

He was assuming, as he always did, that he could claim her time.

Jay nodded, managing a smile. "Why not," she agreed amiably.

As the door closed behind Paul she found her gaze again drawn beyond the office, to the street. Soon she wasn't registering the traffic or the crowds, as her vision drifted inward.

Maybe New York was the solution. Certainly, since returning from Scree Carr, she'd felt unsettled, and was too honest to be unaware of the cause.

Even before she'd completed a third of that long, lonely drive from Yorkshire, she had realized that Rhys couldn't have been responsible for the broken trap door. Enigmatic he may be, dour and irascible perhaps, but he was incapable of harming anyone. She remembered his rescue of the injured bird and his innate respect for all life, however simple. But she also recalled how readily she'd believed the worst of him, and run away.

Granted Rhys could be intimidating. He was very different from Paul, whose fair good looks enabled him to charm his way through life, very different from any man she'd ever known.

She stopped to think. If she didn't blame Rhys for the accident, why was she afraid of him? Was she frightened of the message in his magnetic dark eyes? Of the seemingly inevitable consequence of close contact with a man who aroused in her a longing too intense to ignore; a longing more assertive, more exhilarating, and more wonderful than any she'd previously experienced?

"It isn't only that," she murmured and, noticing that she'd spoken aloud, forced her attention back to her desk.

She opened the catalog she ought to be checking and willed her brain to read. Why was concentration so elusive now? Normally she got through a tremendous work load with an efficiency that had prompted Paul to offer her the New York position. Now, however, she seemed incapable of clearing her mind. If only she weren't so tired . . .

She was sleeping badly. The constant rumble of London traffic, previously acceptable beyond the walls of her apartment, was an acute disturbance now. Each night, she awakened repeatedly, always *listening*. Listening perhaps for the creaking of an old mansion as it settled, for the scraping of a branch against the window, for the waterfall? Or, worse, was she anxiously listening for the moans of someone tormented by a nightmare?

Was Rhys still troubled? Had her hasty departure added to his burdens? She'd handled the situation between them with none of her customary poise. While she'd stayed at Scree Carr, she'd sensed that she was getting through to Rhys, but now . . . ?

If only she could go back to the beginning. It wasn't entirely her fault that she'd reacted badly. Rhys was a mass of contradictions. Everything had happened so quickly, allowing no time to think things through; she'd been attracted long before she'd begun to like him. There was no way to rationalize it though, she shouldn't have panicked.

Jay started guiltily when the door behind her opened. As she turned another page of the catalog, she glanced out of the corner of her eye and saw Avril, their receptionist, and was relieved.

"I'm sorry to bother you, Miss Stanmer, there's a gentleman asking for Mr. Valentine. When I told him he was out, he asked for you."

Jay extended a hand for the business card that Avril was holding.

"I'll see him, of course," she said quickly. "Although I'm not sure that will satisfy . . ." Reading the name on the card, she gulped.

"I'm sure it will," a familiar voice exclaimed from the doorway. "There's no one more likely to satisfy me."

Rhys entered while Jay was coordinating her shaky legs; somehow she struggled to her feet. She composed her features into what she hoped was a smile and reached for the hand he was holding toward her.

His fingers grasped hers firmly, but the expression in his brown eyes was sharper than his smooth words. Jay was aware of the receptionist's curious gaze flicking from one to the other of them.

"Thank you, Avril," she said briskly, "that will be all."

The girl knew to close the door behind her. Jay waited for its click, then inhaled deeply before her eyes leveled with his again.

Rhys smiled ruefully. "Should I allow you time to recover? Maybe I was too precipitate just barging in . . ."

Jay stared at him, emotions surging, preventing coherent thought, let alone speech. He was *here,* as though her longing to set things right had conjured him through space. But he had asked for Paul, *not* for her.

"Yes, you were," she agreed baldly.

"No more than you yourself," he reminded her with equal asperity. "I'd suggested you delay returning to London. I didn't want you to have that long drive. You could at least have telephoned me at the hospital."

"I never even thought of it."

"No." He sounded angry.

Jay shivered, her hand felt icy where his fingers had been withdrawn.

Rhys shrugged and smoothed his already immaculate dark hair.

"I didn't come to quarrel. I thought it fair to advise your boss that Adam Boxley will examine the paintings. You know him, I think."

"Indeed, yes. He's the best, very well respected in the business, as well as outside it. I'm sure he'll prove more than adequate."

"I don't need your confirmation of his credentials," Rhys interjected. "That isn't all, Jay. I came here to suggest that you be present when Adam Boxley gives his verdict."

"I'm not going to change my opinion, you know, no matter what anyone says."

"Even so . . . this is the way I think things should be conducted. If you're so reluctant to come, perhaps Mr. Valentine himself . . ."

"I'm not," she said quickly, interrupting, then she glanced past him, trying to avoid his scrutiny and control her confusion.

"Ah," he observed, then waited for her to speak.

"I . . . I'd have to see what Paul thinks."

"Of course." He seemed to recognize that her boss's possible dissent wasn't involved. "Naturally, I'm offering a substantial fee."

"You think money solves everything, don't you?" Jay snapped, cross because he had the power to manipulate her.

"Alas, no. But it has been known to oil the wheels. I see already that while Valentine might be impressed by a fat fee, you won't be. Not even if it enhances your standing."

Jay was compelled to smile. "I don't know why I bother to say anything. You seem to have weighed all my responses and reactions."

"Accurately?" She experienced the full force of his dark eyes.

For what felt like a long minute, Jay held his gaze. "You're not too far off the mark, sometimes," she said.

Rhys laughed, and all tension evaporated.

"I want you there, Jay. Call it an excuse, if you will, but the invitation's well meant. Please accept it."

She sensed that *please* wasn't a word that appeared frequently in his vocabulary, except perhaps when expecting something of someone he employed.

"You needn't be scared of me," he told her, disarming her completely. "I didn't, and most certainly wouldn't, try to harm you. If you only knew . . ." After a pause he smiled. "I have tickets for a concert at the Albert Hall tonight. Do I have to phone round to all the girls in my little book, or will you come with me? Given the choice, I'd prefer your company."

"You're very gallant all of a sudden," Jay said, smiling back.

"You don't know me in London, do you?"

"Meaning?"

"So far, you've judged me only on what you've seen in that somber place."

"Then I can't refuse, can I?"

"Good. Tell me your address and I'll pick you up at seven. You'll probably want to change after work. If you want to eat something before we go, keep it to a light snack. I know just the spot for supper afterward."

"Won't that be very late?"

Rhys raised an eyebrow. "My dear Jay, you're a sophisticated woman who's lived in London for years. Surely you can manage one late night. Let me prove I can show you a good time."

Again, she had no choice but to laugh. Rhys nodded approvingly. "Until seven o'clock then."

When Paul returned, Jay was tidying her desk. She was shattered by Rhys's unexpected arrival, and more so by his invitation for the evening.

"In a hurry?" asked Paul, frowning.

"Yes, I'm going out."

"I know. I arranged it, didn't I?"

"Oh, no!" Jay exclaimed, aghast. She'd forgotten their plans for the evening.

"Something's come up, has it?" Paul said lightly. "So, okay, we'll make it another night—but soon. We must settle this New York thing."

"Of course. And I'm sorry, Paul, I really had forgotten."

After their last trip abroad, when it had become

obvious that neither of them felt committed, they'd agreed that their dates would remain flexible. But Jay experienced a gnawing suspicion that Paul would be less than delighted about her companion for tonight; and she had to tell him.

"Actually, I'm seeing a client. Rhys Felstead dropped in and—"

"Who?" he roared. She rarely saw Paul so annoyed. Normally easygoing, his fury seemed all the more alarming.

"Rhys—" she repeated, but she got no further.

"I'm not deaf. I wish to God I'd gotten you to New York. Can't you see you're obsessed? It's unhealthy, Jay—totally debilitating. You're not the same person, your work has suffered, your concentration's abysmal. If you don't get him out of your system, you're going to be of no use."

"Well, all right," she retorted. She wasn't far from agreeing. But she resented Paul's intrusion into her private life. "Maybe tonight will end what you term the 'obsession.'"

"Unless you're completely insane, I'll guarantee it will. How you can actually seek his company, I don't know!"

Jay refrained from telling him of the proposed return visit to Scree Carr. If Rhys wanted her there, *he* must convince Paul of the need.

Jay was ready when the Rolls Royce drew up in the mews outside her flat, but only just ready. She'd spent quite a while preparing for the outing. After long deliberation, she'd chosen a skirt and jacket of midnight-blue velvet and a white blouse with a flattering frilled neckline. Even to her own critical gaze, the outfit was pleasing, and as she drew a few blond tendrils toward her face, freeing them from the smooth coil of long hair, she smiled at her reflection. She'd taken infinite pains over her makeup, adding a subtle shading of silvery blue to her eyes, but going easy on the blusher. She was warm already—warmed by excitement, and by delight that she was seeing Rhys.

He was beside the car when she answered the doorbell. His expert glance appraised her appearance as he greeted her. But then he busied himself opening the car door for her and his manner was suddenly so cool that she wondered if she'd imagined his approving look.

"I trust that you enjoy orchestral concerts," he said rather stiffly, getting in beside her and starting the engine.

"As a matter of fact, I love them. Although I'm afraid I neglect music all too often, maybe because good concerts are so readily available."

"Yes."

"If I didn't like this sort of thing, I wouldn't have agreed to go."

"And certainly not with me," he said, rather tetchily.

"Why say that? There were times at Scree Carr when we got on well."

"You shouldn't need to bolt for your life, anyway. Not in public."

Jay felt disturbed that he'd needed to refer yet again to her fears, but she reflected that if she hadn't literally been in danger of being killed, she had been the victim of an incident that she felt sure had *not* been accidental. Whoever had been responsible, though, this certainly wasn't the moment to pursue the matter. She smiled at him.

"I'd been hoping your invitation was proof that you wished to begin again, without the misunderstandings."

Rhys took time over his reply. "Appealing though that concept might be, unfortunately, everything that occurs does have some lasting effect."

Jay sighed. "Rhys, I'm sorry if my impulsive decision to leave your home distressed you. I didn't think it would matter one way or the other."

That wasn't strictly true. She'd suspected that he would be displeased. Was she hoping now that he'd reassure her? Whatever she might have hoped, Rhys said nothing, but turned on the car radio instead, making her wonder if he did regret asking her out.

When he'd parked the car near the Albert Hall, however, he surprised her yet again. As he helped her out he offered his arm and smiled into her eyes.

"You certainly know how to dress for the occasion, Jay. I can't pretend to guess what you spend on clothes, but I've known many a wealthy woman who'd have benefited from your good taste."

"Thank you," she murmured, suddenly realizing that his earlier coolness could have been due to nothing more than shyness.

Briefly, he touched her hand as it rested on his arm. "Maybe you're right, and we can leave the past where it is."

The concert hall was almost full, and Jay glanced all around her as they settled into their seats. "Don't you love the sense of anticipation before a concert," she whispered, "especially in a place this size?"

"I only hope you're not in for a disappointment. Being in town for only a short visit, I couldn't select either the program or the seats."

"Both are just fine," she assured him. As they studied the program notes she scarcely noticed which pieces would be played, because she was so happy to have Rhys beside her. She wished it were possible to hang on to the belief that he was genuinely interested in her, yet she sensed even now that the forbidding chill would again reappear.

For the first time since he'd walked into her office, Jay remembered his visits to the psychiatric hospital. It was likely that whatever caused him to go there could also be responsible for these sudden mood swings. If she wanted their friendship to continue, she would learn to live with that—and today, she felt more than content to do so.

The orchestra had been tuning up. A hush descended as they were joined by their leader, and applause broke out at the conductor's appearance. The vast hall was again filled with anticipatory silence, and Jay drew in a long, happy breath.

The first piece, Mozart's *Eine Kleine Nachtmusik,* was rendered beautifully. As she listened to the familiar strains Jay felt the last touches of awkwardness waning, and she became acutely conscious of the man at her side. She could tell he was also relaxing. At the end of the first movement they exchanged a smile; by the end of the piece she sensed that somehow the music was drawing them together. After the first few bars of Stravinsky's *Rite of Spring,* Rhys found her hand and held it.

The evening passed too quickly. No sooner had an item begun than they were applauding its finish. Jay yearned to hold on to each moment, for Rhys appeared equally happy, and she loved the feel of his hand on hers.

The climax came with Tchaikovsky's *1812* overture, one of Jay's favorites. Although she was familiar with the music, the cannon and mortar effects, close behind them in the auditorium, made her jump violently. Embarrassed, she glanced sideways. Rhys was laughing silently, but she couldn't continue to feel embarrassed;

his laughter was no way sardonic, but simply affectionate amusement. During the final crescendo, his fingers
tightened over hers, and the smile still lingered on his
lips.

Jay thanked him enthusiastically as they walked back
toward his car.

"My pleasure," he responded, his eyes revealing that
the words were far from empty.

As Rhys stopped outside the Kensington restaurant,
Jay smiled to herself. She wouldn't have revealed that
she came here frequently, but the head waiter greeted
her by name as they entered.

Rhys raised an eyebrow. When they'd been shown to
their table, he glanced across, his expression rather
wry.

"It seems I can't teach you much about anything! A
pity. I would have enjoyed introducing you to the
specialties here."

Jay smiled, her gray eyes alight with amusement.
"Sorry to spoil things. But does it matter, since it
proves we have similar tastes?"

"Maybe not. Allow me time to subdue my chauvinis-
tic tendencies."

The meal was a delight. With their shared enjoyment
of the concert, she and Rhys had recaptured their
moments of affinity. When he drove her to her apartment, Jay instinctively asked him in.

"Aren't you being incautious?" he inquired. "Not all
that long ago you considered me a threat."

She was upset, believing he hadn't forgiven her for
running from his home, but then the dashboard light
revealed his lips were twitching.

"Are you laughing at me?" she asked, trying to
sound severe.

"Only because I'm assured we've made that fresh
beginning."

Rhys was interested in her home. While she made coffee, he wandered around the living room, examining her many books, glancing through the records beside the stereo unit, and pausing before every picture. He might have been hoping something would yield a clue to all her secrets.

"Well?" she asked as she returned with a pot of steaming coffee.

He grinned, pretended to look shamefaced, but was too certain of himself to be convincing.

"You thought you'd try to find out what makes me tick, didn't you?"

"You're far too complex for that to be accomplished in a swift appraisal of your environment, but do you object?"

Smiling, she shook her head. "I think I'd be disappointed if you weren't at least curious."

He took his coffee cup but set it aside. Before she could sit down, he held her by the shoulders and gazed earnestly into her eyes.

"I'm more than curious, Jay. I've been happy tonight, happier than I've been for a very long time."

He kissed her then, his hard mouth thrilling her with its insistence. He drew her close against him, and Jay sighed ecstatically, feeling that she was being welcomed back to where she belonged. His lips lingered until she grew short of breath, and the familiar throbbing deep within her made her strain against him. Suddenly, though, Rhys seemed tense. It was only when he continued holding her after his searching mouth left hers that she became aware of the reason. However much he might curtail their kisses, Rhys could not disguise the desire expressed by his taut body, nor still her own eagerness to respond.

He turned from her, reached for his cup, and went to

one of her luxurious armchairs. "Did you speak to Valentine about the proposed visit to Scree Carr?"

"Not yet. He came in only just before I left, and—" She paused, wondering whether to tell him about Paul's annoyance.

"And?" Rhys prompted, frowning, as if he sensed something wrong.

Jay decided to explain. If she wanted Rhys to square the return visit to Yorkshire, he would have to know.

"Paul wasn't too pleased about this evening. You see, I'd forgotten that I'd already arranged to see him."

Rhys checked his smile, but a fraction of a second too late. He took out a slim, leather-covered diary.

"The date I've given Adam Boxley is from May tenth onward. I'll have a word with your boss—assuming you're still willing to come?"

His dark eyes were carefully drained of expression, yet he toyed with the diary pages until Jay answered.

"I'd love to come. I don't like leaving unfinished business anywhere."

Rhys checked another smile, raising an eyebrow.

"Until the paintings get their final verdict, that *is* unfinished," Jay said hastily. Rhys wasn't the only one with reservations about revealing every motive.

"I'll speak to Valentine tomorrow," he said briskly. "I suggest you and I travel on the ninth. Naturally, I expect you to make the journey in comfort, in my car."

Jay readily agreed. A quiver of excitement coursed through her as she anticipated traveling with him. She felt like a lighthearted teenager, for once, instead of a woman of twenty-six.

The ninth was dry and sunny, a perfect day for a car journey through the English countryside. As soon as the Rolls had quietly devoured the busy London roads and they were heading along the motorway, Jay's spirits soared. Rhys hadn't confided how he'd persuaded Paul to agree to her coming, and she hadn't inquired. He was very relaxed again, talking of the auction he'd attended at Christie's the previous week, then exclaiming about the fresh green of the fields and meadows, and generally delighting her.

"Are you glad to get away from London?" Jay asked.

He shrugged. "In some ways perhaps, though I'm the first to acknowledge that London's the place to be if you care about any of the arts. And, of course, there's nowhere quite like the Albert Hall," he added, making her smile.

"It was a good evening, wasn't it?" she enthused, relieved. When Rhys hadn't asked her out again during his stay, she'd wondered what was wrong.

They stopped for luncheon near Stratford-upon-Avon, where he led the way into a country hotel. "Generally, I don't eat much during a journey, but you should order whatever you want."

"I've never thought that traveling and eating heavily combined very well, so I'll be guided by you," Jay said.

"Have you been here before?"

"Never," she assured him, laughing mischievously. "Do indulge your longing to show me what's what."

They ate a Special Plowman's Lunch, which turned out to be not only the expected cheese and crusty French bread, but all kinds of cold meats, pâté, and a generous salad garnish.

Rhys offered wine but Jay preferred lager. She didn't hear his order and when the drinks arrived, his own choice proved to be a brimming tankard of beer.

Her surprised amusement must have been less contained than Jay supposed. Rhys gazed at her, and one long finger teased the corner of her lips.

"Why not laugh?" he said, his brown eyes warm.

"Your expression labels the pint of beer uncharacteristic, but I am a Yorkshireman. Shouldn't I like good bitter?"

Jay smiled, but said nothing.

"You think I'm a bit of an enigma."

"I'm beginning to wonder if you enjoy being one."

"Ah." He smiled to himself yet again. "Yes, well. You'd better get on with your snack and curtail the analysis."

"But Rhys isn't exactly a Yorkshire name, is it?"

"True. A quarter of me is Welsh, and my grandmother's family had a Rhys in each generation. Blame the Celtic blood for the colorful moods."

Jay was having difficulty remembering that this was the man whose dour welcome and brusque manner once had made her ache to escape his home. Today, she knew Rhys was happy simply enjoying their day.

She was all the more disappointed when, as they approached the moors surrounding his home, his mood darkened noticeably. He hardly spoke at all, and gave monosyllabic answers to her questions.

As he swung the Rolls Royce into the drive of Scree Carr, a frown wrinkled his forehead, and the dark eyes hardened. She longed to be able to alleviate his tension, and remembered he was the one who should have been putting her at ease. Why couldn't he unwind at his own home?

The front door was opened by a large, middle-aged woman whose severe face thawed when she saw Rhys.

"Jay, this is my housekeeper, Mrs. Godfrey, whom you didn't meet during your previous stay. Mrs. Godfrey—Miss Stanmer. I believe you've prepared the tapestry room again? Please show her up."

The housekeeper, if somewhat forbidding, was well trained; she inquired after their journey, remarked on the weather, and said she hoped Jay would enjoy her visit. When they reached the room that Jay recalled so vividly, Mrs. Godfrey surprised her, smiling and crossing to the window, then indicating the view over the grounds of the estate.

"You'll doubtless find a big change in the scenery, Miss Stanmer. I understand you'd a lot of snow here before. You'd not be as used to that as we are."

"That's true, although the snow and ice created their own kind of beauty."

"Yes. But it's the harm ice does that we mustn't forget, and the way it chills everything so. This old house needs sunshine. Not that we don't love the place. I'm almost as fond of it as the master is."

"But—" Jay began, and hastily bit back her remark. She'd been about to say that Rhys seemed anything but happy here.

Mrs. Godfrey read her expression anyway, and sighed. "You've noticed he doesn't seem happy here, haven't you? We do our best, but we don't seem able to help. Some who come here can't stand his manner. They don't understand him." She paused, looking at Jay, weighing her. "But you're different. You want to understand, don't you?"

Jay was taken aback. "Well, yes, I . . . yes." She smiled. "Perhaps between us, Mrs. Godfrey, we'll do some good."

"I hope so, Miss Stanmer, I do hope so."

Before they could say any more, Rhys called Mrs. Godfrey. Left alone, Jay remained by the window, looking out, saddened that Rhys wasn't able to fully appreciate such a beautiful home. She ached to help him accept whatever caused these black moods . . . to make him happy. Mrs. Godfrey was more concerned for him than Jay had imagined. She could, indeed, be the very person to help.

Jay became aware of his voice beyond the door, which had been left ajar.

". . . so I want you to go there tomorrow. I want that London flat smartened up, Mrs. Godfrey, and no one but you can take charge of that."

Jay's spirit's plummeted. He was sending the house-keeper away. She herself, *alone,* would have to find some way of restoring his equilibrium.

She turned to glance around the room, her own emotions far from stable. Deep down she was very glad to be back here, seeing the exquisite furnishings with a new awareness and undisguised affection. And yet already she was dreading the apprehensions that would come with the night.

Chapter Five

"Did you say Adam Boxley is arriving tomorrow?"

"Yes."

"So Mrs. Harper will have three of us to look after."

"Boxley won't be sleeping here. I've booked him into the local hotel."

"Oh." Jay was astonished; she'd assumed one of the many empty rooms would have been put to use.

Rhys smiled wryly. "Do you need a chaperon?"

Color flared in her cheeks. "Not in the least, only . . ."

"I can't think why you should," he observed, calmly. "My behavior the other evening was impeccable—the epitome of restraint."

Jay didn't know what on earth to say. *She* had spent a restless night after the concert, aware of him still, because he'd reawakened all of the desire that he'd aroused previously. And Rhys had been equally in need of her, yet he'd called a halt to their kisses.

Wasn't he trying now to provoke her into revealing what she'd felt? She wasn't about to give any hint of the exciting and quite alarming effect he always had on her while he remained so contained.

"You don't seem very relieved that, at thirty-five,

I've enough sense to spare you the grand seduction routine," he persisted, and Jay noticed his secret smile and knew he was teasing her.

Quite suddenly, though, she realized that in abandoning all restraint he could, somehow, be released from whatever bonds the past and this house imposed upon him. And she longed to be the one to make him forget everything but their present, and future.

"Or are you afraid of something far more menacing?" he demanded.

He was scowling, the eyes behind the lenses harsh. They'd just finished dinner, an excellent meal that they both had enjoyed. Why was he already spoiling things?

Abruptly, Jay rose, wanting to get away for a while. She felt oppressed by him, and confused by the illogicality of her own instincts, which seemed to be galloping ahead of her.

"I'm sorry. If you'll excuse me, I am rather tired. The journey—"

"Don't lie to me."

Rhys was swift. Before she'd taken three paces he was at her side, his hand firm upon her arm. All at once she felt frightened. He was very tall. Though slender he possessed powerful shoulders and the strength of the fingers detaining her seemed implacable.

"*Are* you scared, Jay? Afraid that I've contrived very conveniently to rid us of the company that might protect you? You know I'm sending Mrs. Godfrey to London, and I'm arranging for Boxley to sleep in the village; you're aware Amy Harper doesn't live in—"

"You're trying to frighten me. Why? You're actually trying to make me wonder if you're planning to hurt me."

"Or ensuring that you examine such fears and dismiss them as ludicrous?" He released her arm, but held her with his gaze, the dark eyes plumbing her soul. His voice softened, although his expression didn't alter. "I've said already, Jay, that I'd never harm you; but I can't force you to believe me."

"I . . . just don't understand you," she admitted reluctantly. And knew how she ached to learn.

"That's no surprise. No one has."

He turned from her then, and intuition screamed that she mustn't let him walk away out of the room.

"Rhys—"

He glanced back when he reached the door.

"I think I should get a turn now," Jay said firmly. "You've said what you wanted. If we're being frank, surely that can only do good."

He smiled at her approach, then shrugged and crossed to the sideboard. "Join me in a brandy?"

Rhys brought her glass over, then indicated huge leather armchairs to either side of the hearth. "You may as well sit in comfort while you endure the discomfort of trying to get along with me!"

Jay laughed, although moments ago she'd have thought laughing unlikely. He really was an astonishing person.

"Rhys Felstead, you enjoy perplexing people, don't you?"

"My dear Jay, how can I know? It's a part of me, I guess, not always consciously assumed. But it was your turn for holding forth."

"You make me forget what I was going to say."

"Glad I'm getting through to you, at least."

"Stop it!" she exclaimed. She might enjoy his chatting her up, but there was something quite serious that she had to say.

"Rhys—how can you expect me to trust you, when you don't trust anyone?"

He'd been staring absently into the goblet warming between cupped hands, but at her words his head

jerked up and his gaze sought hers. He raised one dark
eyebrow, as he did so often, but didn't speak.

"You don't let anyone in, or never more than
fleetingly."

"So? Forget me." He paused. "Running away isn't
like you, Jay, I have to stop you. Run from me, if you
must, though I'd prefer that you didn't, but not from
life; that's no solution."

"But you don't trust me, do you?" she persisted.

"Because I'm having someone substantiate your professional opinion?"

"I'm not talking about the paintings."

Rhys swallowed; he could have been containing
anger, annoyance, even amusement. Eventually, just
as the silence was growing unendurable, he spoke,
looking hard into the brandy again, avoiding her scrutiny.

"I'll admit one thing, Jay—once I'd have acknowledged freely that I enjoy your company, that we seem
so well attuned that we oughtn't to waste such rare
affinity. But that was once . . ."

A question, nagging away for days, had to be answered. "Are you married?"

He shook his head. "No, I never have been."

"Committed to someone then?"

"No—not now—and never will be again."

The assertion seemed as cold as the snow which once
had surrounded Scree Carr; yet she sensed that Rhys
himself was saddened. What was so terribly wrong?

"So, we're both free," Jay said, managing a smile
when he glanced toward her. "Let's enjoy what comes,
without provoking each other—and without repeated
reminders that I made a mistake one time and ran
away."

To her delight, Rhys smiled back. "Let's drink to
that."

She rose as he approached. He made a ceremony of their toast, linking their arms, sipping from her glass, offering his own. When their gaze met, some wordless message lingering in his brown eyes caught her to him.

Rhys took her glass and set them both down, then drew her close. "You're here again, Jay. I'll try to make you as glad as I am." He kissed her hair, eyelids, and cheek, and then his lips found hers, moving over them, willing her to respond. And responding was all too easy, it was restraint that Jay was finding difficult. She heard his quickening breath and felt the urgent pulsing of his heart against her, but then he sighed.

"Maybe you're right about the journey being tiring. Have your brandy in your room," he suggested, and the firelight gleamed in the golden liquid as he handed it across. When she glanced at him he smiled.

"Yes, I did want to make you aware of me when you first came here," he said. The look in his dark eyes confirmed what they both knew—that he'd succeeded far beyond expectations, to the extent of creating a mutual attraction very difficult to ignore.

Gently, he kissed her again, and smiled. "I don't regret any of this Jay, but—"

"—things developed a little too quickly to allow much time for thought?" Jay suggested, quite lightly, but as she turned and walked slowly toward the door, she was feeling bereft.

"Sleep well, love," Rhys said, surprising her by the endearment.

Without the icy winds, Scree Carr was still tormented by sufficient breeze to rattle the panes and whistle in the chimneys. Jay lay there, listening; beyond the immediate vicinity of the house, she could hear the waterfall, tumultuous as her emotions.

Learning that Rhys had previously set out to attract her made her all the more perplexed. It seemed as though she were being allowed a glimpse of Rhys as he might once have been, before whatever trauma had made him wary of deepening relationships. She wished so very much that she could have known him then, for she was sure he'd have been consistently warmhearted as well as hot-blooded. With each meeting she came to know him better, and she could appreciate that she wasn't alone in feeling, as well as wanting, far more than desire. Never in her life had she so longed to be closer to another person.

Jay was still sleepless hours later when she heard the first moans from the room across the landing. She remembered his visits to the psychiatric hospital and realized that it might be likely that the need for treatment was enough to prevent him from tying himself to anyone. *And,* she thought, the dark, nighttime dread increasing her panic, there could be other secret troubles here. He'd warned her once of some danger within the house. She'd believed then that the only danger was of their own physical needs assuming control. But wasn't it possible that the threat was of something far more terrible?

Rhys possessed a mind far sharper than her own. Could he be cunning, capable of convincing someone of whatever he wished them to believe? Had he, only tonight, been doubly clever in contriving to have her alone with him and, by airing and dismissing her possible fears, created a false sense of security?

No sooner had these awful possibilities arisen to distress her than Jay heard the moans again. Alert, each limb stiffening, she listened. But all the while her ears were straining, she felt fright waning and being supplanted by an overwhelming concern for Rhys. When she heard the click of his door opening, she paused only to slip on slippers and her housecoat before following.

When she opened her own door, the only light was from the moon, slanting through an uncurtained window to lick the white painted sides of each step. Sensing that Rhys had gone downstairs, she followed.

Reaching the hall which seemed enormous in the gloom, she hesitated, glancing about her, wondering where he'd gone. None of the rooms showed any glimmer of light. She had just decided that she must have mistaken his direction when she shivered and gazed toward the draft. An outside door stood ajar—the door Rhys kept locked.

Drawing her robe more tightly about her, Jay crossed the hall. The moon had retreated behind a cloud, and she stood a long while, blinking, before she could distinguish the deeper darkness of the shrubbery. Then she stepped out into the chill night air and gazed all around, bewitched by the contrast of the starry sky above her head and the black mansion behind. It was a moment before she saw Rhys.

He didn't start when she reached his side. He'd been aware of her approach, although her thin soles made no sound over the paving. Before she could speak, his arm went about her shoulders, gathering her to his side, astonishing her, though she sensed already that being with him was right.

He was facing toward the waterfall. Out here its sound, plummeting through the chasm, was louder, almost menacing. After a minute Jay felt him sigh.

"I disturbed you again," he said wearily. "Perhaps I shouldn't have asked you to come."

"Am I complaining? I didn't have to come."

Through his robe and her own, Rhys was icily cold.

"Do you want a hot drink?" she suggested. "I could use one. I think I can still remember where the things are kept."

His arm tightened appreciatively and remained

around her shoulders until he paused to lock the door after them when they went indoors. He followed quite slowly when she headed toward the kitchen, and Jay felt his dark gaze pressing at her back.

Rhys still was pensive as he sat at the kitchen table while she made hot chocolate. But when she gave him the mug, he looked up, meeting her eyes with an intensity that belied the chill of his muttered thanks. A little wary of the attraction that so frequently sparked between them, Jay was about to go past and sit at the breakfast bar, but Rhys caught her wrist and drew her down onto the chair beside his.

"Whether or not Adam Boxley confirms that the paintings are forged, I'm going to sell them," he announced abruptly. "Of course, if they were genuine, I could get more for them, but I'll sell them anyway. I'm already planning to get rid of several items from my collection, as you know. I want to buy others, and I need space."

"That sounds interesting . . ." Jay began, not certain whether to say any more.

Rhys shrugged. "I'll keep the family portraits, those pictures connected specifically with the house, and one or two others I'm particularly fond of, like the Degas."

"And what will you buy? Is there something special you've seen?"

He grinned dolefully. "I'm not nearly so sure what I want. No, Jay, I'm just certain that I've got to make some changes here, at last."

"You won't sell the paintings in my room, will you?" she asked impulsively.

He smiled, sipped the hot drink, then raised an eyebrow at her as he set down the mug. "*Your* room?"

"I'm sorry. I mean the tapestry room."

His expression became a curious mixture of amusement and regret.

"I was teasing," he said lightly. "I'm glad you feel at home; surprised as well. But keeping a room as it is can be a mistake."

"Like that room at the top of the house?"

Rhys sighed, took another sip, and looked at her.

"There's no point in pretending, is there? We both know it's a gloomy place."

Jay wondered if she was going to learn the full reason why the room disturbed him, but he rose abruptly, drained the chocolate, and pushed back the chair so sharply that it rocked on its legs.

"Lord knows what the time is!"

"Time we tried again to sleep, I guess," Jay said, emptying her own mug, then crossing to the sink.

He left the kitchen while her back was turned, and Jay was surprised when he was waiting at the foot of the stairs. They went up, side by side, in silence. She was afraid she'd been unable to do any good, yet when they reached the landing Rhys took her gently by the arm, and drew her to him. His kiss was brief, but firm nevertheless; a delicious possession of her lips that affirmed their growing understanding.

"For not questioning me," he said, and was gone.

"So, he hasn't put you in this room then?" Adam Boxley remarked, tugging at the pointed artist's beard which, like his hair, was as blond as her own head. He laughed sharply.

Jay had joined him upstairs to reexamine the paintings.

"Felstead made such a point of keeping you to himself, I thought he was using you to lay the ghost."

"You mean the tragedy of his great-grandfather's bride?"

"I don't mean that at all," Boxley interrupted, his keen blue eyes glinting with amusement. "I see the master of the house hasn't confided very much. However, let's finalize the business and escape this room. Whatever its source, there's no doubting the pervading misery."

Boxley passed from one painting to the next, giving them only a cursory glance because, as he'd said, he'd already reached his conclusion.

"He won't like learning they're forgeries," he said, then smiled over his shoulder. "But then, I gather he's been told. For once, you were right."

He paused when Jay inhaled sharply. She'd never liked Boxley, who was a prejudiced antifeminist and couldn't resist an excuse to put down any woman, no matter how skilled.

"Thank you," she said sarcastically, her head inclining in a mock bow. Boxley didn't miss the loathing in her gray eyes.

"Sorry," he said, but without sincerity.

Jay shrugged. "I'm not here to please you either. Paul will be glad you support my verdict, that's all I care about."

"Really? It doesn't worry you then that Felstead will have his last lingering illusions about these pictures shattered?"

Her smile was wry. "I think he's already convinced they're faked."

"Then why waste money on a second opinion?"

"Pigheadedness? We're all prone to that at times."

"I'm surprised you admit to the possibility that he could be."

"Oh?" she said, her tone just as biting as his had been.

Boxley grinned, an infuriating know-it-all look in his steady blue eyes. "Don't pretend you haven't succumbed. I've watched you watching him during those subdued luncheons we've suffered in that morgue of a room. And you always support him in our conversations."

"What conversations?" Jay scoffed. "You and I have scarcely exchanged twenty sentences." She disliked Boxley, so she kept each encounter brief.

He laughed. "What you've said then has been singularly revealing."

She sighed irritably. "Have you finished in here? We'd better tell Mr. Felstead, hadn't we? Shall we issue the verdict together?"

"Either way, it's immaterial to me. Since he's had your opinion once, there's no need for you to reiterate it. I thought you might be glad to spare him if you could."

"I don't know what you're getting at," Jay said hastily. But she was annoyed when, under his scrutiny, hot color flooded her cheeks.

"All right," he said, in a conciliatory tone. "I'll stop baiting you. Your concern could be no more than interest in a client. In this instance, maybe sympathy is justified. You know, of course, why Felstead is so disturbed that their authenticity is questioned?" he asked, nodding toward the paintings.

"He shows the natural concern of any serious collector."

"You *don't* know, do you?" Amazement drained his voice of arrogance. He looked for one last time toward the paintings, then nodded toward the door. "You ought to be told, without delay."

"Never mind me, I think *Rhys* ought to be told your decision."

"He's out, isn't he? At the psychiatric place."

"Is he? I didn't know this was one of his days for treatment."

As they started down the stairs Jay felt Boxley's curious glance. Since he evidently knew where Rhys went when he was absent from Scree Carr, she couldn't think what she had said that warranted that look.

"Has he never told you the history of those paintings then?" Adam Boxley asked conversationally, as they descended the staircase.

"No, and I didn't think it was my concern. I gathered that they weren't purchased through any of the approved dealers though."

"They were a gift."

Jay stood still, thinking, as they gained the hall. "But if he didn't buy them why is he so disturbed that they're not authentic?"

"That's what I'm going to tell you . . . now that you're showing interest." He glanced toward first the lounge, then the front door. "Care for a stroll? This house gives me the creeps—I'll be thankful to have a bit of fresh air."

Boxley continued as soon as they were walking over the wide lawn surrounding the mansion. "I know why Felstead is perturbed. Thosepaintings were a wedding present, from his fiancée."

"I didn't know he was engaged," Jay began, then stopped, awkwardly. This was what Rhys had meant when he mentioned some previous commitment. But before she'd absorbed its significance, Boxley interrupted her thoughts.

"He is playing with his cards tight against his chest. But then, I don't imagine he'll be much given to confidences. And I wouldn't have been aware of his engagement either, if my original visit here hadn't been canceled so abruptly. On account of her death."

"Oh, God! Does that mean it was sudden?"

"I really don't know. I received a message canceling the arrangement because of a bereavement. I assumed he'd lost some aged relative until I read the paragraph in *The Times.*"

"But how did she die?"

"There may have been some accident. I don't know, I wasn't particularly interested. I'm not now. In any case, I went abroad then. If there'd been anything further in the papers, I wouldn't have known."

"But you knew she'd given Rhys the paintings."

"I made it my business to find out. After he'd contacted me again, the other week. I thought I'd better learn all I could since even he was admitting they could be faked."

"And the girl, who was she?"

"Sheila Danby."

The name meant nothing to Jay. Boxley smiled to himself again.

"You don't get around very much, do you?"

"Meaning I should have known her? Paul and I travel together a lot, but mostly in Europe and the States. He generally covers the British stuff himself."

"I'll enlighten you yet again. Sheila Danby was the only daughter of Sir Charles and Lady Danby, neighbors of the Felsteads, and equally loaded."

"So she and Rhys were old friends."

"On the contrary. Apparently Sheila had lived in Paris for years. She and Felstead only became reacquainted when her mother was ill and she returned to England. Lady Danby recovered, but Sheila stayed on. I gather she'd set her cap at Felstead, as the saying goes, and wasn't prepared to let go."

"He wouldn't be trapped by some female if he wasn't willing."

"Agreed. But I've seen a portrait; believe me, any man would have to be made of ice to remain immune. And they say the strong silent types topple all the harder when they fall."

"But the bit about her haunting that room in the house. You invented that, didn't you? You couldn't know anything if this is your first visit."

"You don't want to know, do you? I've no need to invent such a thing. There's already plenty that's macabre here. I happen to know that Sheila insisted on sleeping in that room during her frequent visits. The friend who put me wise on the source of those paintings knew that Felstead was, apparently, worried by his fiancée's somewhat morbid interest in the earlier bride."

"It sounds depressing, but it doesn't really concern us, does it?" Jay wanted to be rid of Boxley, to be alone, so she could consider all that she'd learned about Rhys. Was his fiancée's death the reason he needed psychiatric help?

Preoccupied, she started when a crackling of the undergrowth at the far side of the hedge interrupted her thoughts. The man who straightened his back and continued trimming the hedge proved to be Mike Travers, and she had to control a shudder. Although this was their first encounter since her return, she'd caught glimpses of him about the grounds, a menacing presence, reminding her of the fright he'd given her earlier.

Concealing her aversion, she was about to greet the gardener when he pointedly turned his back. Before Jay had overcome her annoyance at what had seemed like a deliberate snub, Boxley continued speaking. "Well, I'll be only too happy to confirm that those pictures are faked, and be on my way. Since you assure me you're not personally involved with Felstead, I take it you'd like a lift back to London?"

"I don't know," Jay hedged, reluctant to leave, and very reluctant to believe that Rhys's sole reason for inviting her had been a business one.

Realizing that she'd sounded unenthusiastic, she managed a smile.

"I'm sorry, that was ungrateful, but Mr. Felstead said he might want me to advise him on other paintings now that I'm here."

"I see." He grinned. "Well, I shall be off first thing tomorrow. If you want a ride, ring me at the hotel before, say, eight o'clock."

They turned and began to walk back toward the front entrance.

"But I'll see you at dinner tonight, won't I?" Jay said. "I understand Mrs. Harper is going to lay on something special."

He grimaced. "Then he'll expect me there. In case we have no opportunity for a private word, I ought to caution you: If you're not involved already with Felstead, steer clear. He's a strange individual, and I'd trust him about as far as I could shift that great pile of a mansion. In some ways, you know, I sympathize with Sheila Danby—you could live with him for years without being able to begin to guess what he was thinking. One can't help believing she escaped a more unpleasant fate."

Jay swallowed, took a deep breath, and swallowed again. She would not rise to Boxley's words, which she considered grossly unfair.

In her room she sat staring out over the extensive grounds, feeling more than ever that she wanted to stay. Surely her instinct to like Rhys, despite his initial coolness, hadn't been misguided. And with everything that she learned, his behavior became more understandable. She could see now why he was reluctant to welcome any other woman here, why he didn't trust people—or didn't trust fate sufficiently to allow himself to care about anyone again.

Jay glimpsed her own reflection, gazing back from

the mirror that hung between the windows and, slowly, rose and walked toward the glass.

Her eyes appeared darker than usual, their liquid silver turned to steel by the intensity of her concern. But there was nothing of steel's hardness in the film of tears which briefly dulled her vision. Unless Rhys told her to leave, she wouldn't travel to London tomorrow, nor the next day.

On hearing of his love for the woman he had lost, she'd recognized how much she cared about him. She couldn't go while there was hope that by remaining, she might help.

All at once, she ached quite fiercely to see him. She longed to make up for whatever the past had done, and allow him to be himself again—even amusing. And affectionate? she wondered, and sighed.

Brushing out her hair after she had bathed, Jay decided to leave it loose about her shoulders. She loved to feel its pale silkiness drifting against her skin, and tonight she'd no need to cling to the businesslike image which so often prompted her to adopt a more severe style. She neither knew nor cared if Adam Boxley acknowledged her professional authority. And Rhys? She smiled wryly. She'd been speaking the truth earlier when she'd said she believed Rhys accepted her expertise. Tonight, that aspect was the last thing to concern her.

She had dressed carefully before for Rhys, but now she took infinite care. The dress she chose was very simple, a subtle lavender which Paul once said conjured from her eyes a similar shade. As she slipped into the soft, crepe material, she wondered fleetingly if its low neckline and lack of sleeves might be cool here even in May. Somehow, she just didn't care. She felt right in the dress, she decided, adjusting its draped bodice, and she sensed Rhys would approve its simplicity.

Ruefully, she began applying mascara to her fair lashes. It was only very rarely, these days, that she dressed to please any man. But as far as she knew there might only be tonight, and with Boxley holding forth, she couldn't count on keeping her host's attention. As she checked her reflection yet again before going down, Jay noted that Rhys had scarcely been out of her thoughts all day. Nor, indeed, since her previous visit to his home. It had been a long time since anyone had held her interest for so long.

He was waiting in the hall, in the same place he'd stood on her first visit. His expression as she came down the long staircase seemed equally forbidding. And now that summer was approaching and there was only a token blaze from the logs in the hearth, the thin glow of firelight failed to soften the sharpness of his features.

Jay felt deep within her a tug of an anxiety that she knew she couldn't voice.

"I'm the first then, am I?" she said lightly, glancing around for Boxley.

Rhys started as he glanced up and she realized that he'd been too preoccupied to hear her coming. She wanted to go to him and slip her arm through his, to smile at him and talk, and ease away his frown. But then the frown vanished without her intervention, and he came toward her, a hand outstretched.

"You're very lovely," he said, his eyes paying her extravagant compliments while they absorbed each detail of her ensemble, her gently draped gown, her sandaled feet.

His fingers closed on hers and, smiling, he raised her hand to his lips. "I'm sure my ancestors would approve my approval!" he exclaimed, his glance briefly flicking toward the portraits on the wall, half-amused by his own gallantry.

Jay smiled into his eyes, feeling inexpressibly warmed. When the dark gaze continued to hold her own, straying no farther than the cascade of hair that tumbled against her high cheekbones, she felt her heartbeat quicken.

"Need I say I'm glad you're the first—that I wish, crazily, that I'd let Boxley dine at the hotel? And may I ask you now if you have to leave tomorrow?"

Jay smiled, delighted by how much he cared.

"Well, I said nothing to Paul about when I'd return to London. And you did mention other paintings you'll be offering for auction."

He seized her lead. "Yes, I do require advice, perhaps a sounding board for some of my ideas. And when you were here before you saw nothing of our countryside. I'd love to show you my favorite haunts."

"And I'd love that, Rhys."

His smile deepened, and he looked around, checking that they were still alone. "I was going to suggest you return for a long weekend, but I don't want you to go away. If you don't have to hurry back, take a short vacation now. Afterward, we'll talk pictures and naturally, I'll pay for your time."

She smiled up at him. "Forget the money, Rhys. I'll enjoy helping in whatever capacity I can."

"Ah, but while I'm paying you, Valentine won't complain, or expect you back."

"You seem to have thought this through very thoroughly," she remarked, hardly believing that Rhys so readily accommodated her longing to remain.

He shrugged, dismissively. "One tries."

"We'll sort out the details later, but I'll certainly promise not to dash away."

Rhys glanced toward the grandfather clock, took out an antique gold pocket watch, and verified the time.

"Boxley's late. Have you seen him since this afternoon?"

"Not since we were discussing the paintings. Haven't you?"

"I thought he was coming straight to my study when I returned. In fact, I left the hospital early, but there was no sign of him."

"How strange." Jay sighed, understanding how anxiously Rhys must be awaiting Boxley's verdict. She wished the wretched man would turn up so the business could be settled.

"He's condemned them as faked, hasn't he?" Rhys said sharply.

When she hesitated to confirm it, he laughed wryly.

"You needn't hesitate. He as good as told me earlier, and I've known in my own mind, anyway, that you weren't wrong."

His faith in her opinion didn't cheer. "I'm sorry, Rhys," she whispered, a lump rising in her throat. It must matter terribly to him that his fiancée's gift had proved so deceptive.

He surprised her by smiling again. "You said that when you told me; then it helped. Today the whole affair seems to matter less. I'll just be very glad when I'm shot of every wretched one." He strolled across and picked up the telephone receiver. "I think he must have gone to the hotel to change. I'll hurry him along."

Boxley hadn't returned to the hotel. Rhys frowned, puzzled, then sent Mrs. Harper to see if he was taking another look at the paintings. Afterward he smiled apologetically.

"Even now that I'm trying to act the attentive host, I'm not very convincing. Forgive me, Jay, I should have offered you a drink as soon as you appeared. What'll you have?"

"A sherry perhaps, I don't really mind." She felt too elated to care what she drank.

"If you don't particularly want sherry, let me mix you a cocktail. I do a very good whisky sour."

"Do you now?" Jay was amused. She would never have believed he enjoyed entertaining sufficiently to learn the intricacies of mixing cocktails.

"Find yourself a seat," he said.

Jay enjoyed watching Rhys adroitly preparing the lemon, and his long fingers handling the shaker. She smiled when he walked over with her glass.

"Thank you. It's nice having you wait on me."

He laughed. "Make the most of it. I'm more accustomed to having others attend to my needs. I've brought in Mrs. Godfrey's nieces to help. Doesn't that prove I can't survive without a housekeeper? And *hospitality?* It's some time since I practiced the art."

Her smile vanished. She wanted to tell him that she understood, that she'd learned a little about his fiancée, and was sorry. But she wasn't sorry, was she? She couldn't wish Sheila Danby alive. She herself would have no place here, no chance at all of . . . of what? What did she want?

"Hey now, what's wrong?" Rhys reproved her gently, but was interrupted by Amy Harper, breathless from climbing up and down the stairs.

"I'm sorry, sir, I can't find Mr. Boxley. I've looked in that room, and I took the liberty of knocking on the door of each guest bathroom."

"Not to worry," he said smoothly. "We won't delay any further, Mrs. Harper; you may serve dinner immediately."

Smiling, Rhys glanced down at Jay. "Come along, and bring your drink with you."

Jay had finished her whisky sour when the exquisitely presented first course was served. She glanced at Rhys as she took up her fork. "You choose your staff most effectively. If I hadn't known Mrs. Godfrey was your housekeeper, I'd never have guessed her deputy had prepared this meal."

He grinned. "I'm a lazy man, Jay, I have to surround myself with efficiency. But I am fortunate. Those two are a loyal pair."

"I'm glad. I wouldn't like to think of you in this great place without someone to look after you."

"I said lazy, not helpless," he reminded her, still smiling.

"That's not really the point, is it?"

"No? You mean Scree Carr is so somber it needs an ample supply of the creature comforts to make it bearable?"

"Well . . ."

"You don't like the house, do you?" Without the spectacles, his gaze seemed inescapable, boring into her, willing the truth from her lips.

"Sometimes I feel it's menacing, but it's most likely my imagination. I don't know," Jay said, and wished he would leave the matter alone.

Rhys appeared to reach a decision. "And you said you wouldn't probe. Don't. And certainly not to-night."

Something in his expression seemed to close against her; he meant the warning. If she began prying into the past, she could uncover something more disturbing than what she already knew. Suddenly she shivered, as if the icy winds tormenting Scree Carr during her previous visit were wafting through the ill-fitting windows. She glanced over her shoulder to the darkness gathering in the corners of the room.

"One moment." Rhys took from his pocket a heavy gold lighter and lit each candle in the candelabra. "Better?"

She nodded. "Take no notice of me. You've a lovely home, Rhys."

"And yet—" he said weightily, and sighed. "I know, Jay. But let's forget all the things that are wrong and think instead of the candlelight on your hair, making it gleam like . . . like . . . well, poetry never was my forte."

She laughed gently. "No? You had me convinced! But I thought you weren't trying to turn my head."

"And if I was wrong to be so overcautious, Jay? Supposing I assert myself, and try proving my wishes might be yours, what then?"

"Good question," she said ruefully. "Are you surprised if I admit to being rather bewildered? You're like two people, you know," she began, and checked herself, all lightheartedness banished. Being like two people had a name, hadn't it—schizophrenia.

"Ah, but the better of the two always responds to you!"

Somehow, Jay couldn't dismiss the shadow that had spoiled their evening. She was glad when Mrs. Harper came to take their dishes and serve the main course.

"There's a bit of a mystery about Mr. Boxley, sir," the daily woman announced with evident enjoyment. "The hotel manager's just rung up to ask if he's here, after all. Someone's been trying to get through to him from London, and he isn't anywhere in the hotel."

Rhys shrugged. "As you can see, he's not here, Mrs. Harper. You yourself searched the rest of the house."

When they were alone, Jay turned anxiously toward him. "He'll be all right, won't he? I mean, nothing can have happened to him, can it?"

Rhys laughed at her alarm. "You're letting the atmosphere get to you; aren't you? Forget him, love— unless you're wishing he were here?"

"Don't be silly."

"Well, I for one rejoice that he's disappeared."

"And you don't think we ought to . . . report he's missing?"

"To whom, the police? If you insist, I won't prevent you. But I can't think they'll attach much importance to a grown man going off for the night. He's probably taken up with somebody local."

"But surely he's a married man?"

"You are an innocent, aren't you? Doesn't being off the leash, miles from home, add incentive?"

Despite Rhys's amusement, and his ready dismissal of her concern, Jay couldn't quite submerge her own uneasiness. The evening seemed wasted, distressingly so when she reflected that there was no guarantee that Rhys would ever again prove so gallant. When they'd finished eating, she was feeling irrationally disturbed. Before eleven o'clock she was professing that she was tired, and saying good night.

Rhys seemed astonished and more than a little disappointed. If it hadn't been for her misgivings about Boxley, she'd have been delighted by his ill-concealed desire to prolong their evening, but the day had been tiring. And she not only wanted to think about the mystery of Adam Boxley, but she also needed time alone to reexamine all that she'd heard about Rhys himself.

She was halfway up the staircase when Rhys answered the telephone in the hall.

"That was Mrs. Boxley," he called up to her, after a very brief conversation. "You see, she's checking up on him. What do you bet that he's made the most of his absences from home before?"

Chapter Six

At seven-thirty the next morning Jay telephoned the hotel and asked for Adam Boxley. There was no answer from his room, and the receptionist confirmed that he hadn't returned the previous night.

During breakfast, Jay was upset, wondering if she should tell Rhys, yet sensing he'd be annoyed because she hadn't accepted his theory. They were eating in the dining room, which felt cold, its pervading gloom as chilling as the physical temperature. Even when Rhys suggested that they begin her vacation by driving over the moors toward the sea, she had difficulty in sharing his enthusiasm.

"Are you still worrying about that fellow?" He sounded irritated. "I may not scintillate, but I hoped I'd take your mind off him; especially since he's married, and you evidently consider that relationship sacrosanct."

"I'm only afraid he might have had an accident," she

said hurriedly, sorry that he saw her concern for Boxley as a personal affront.

Rhys grinned piteously. "And I'm only showing the resentment of the human male who's deprived of complete attention! Come on, let's make the most of our day."

Away from the house, Jay let go all her worries, and Rhys became an engaging companion whose alert mind was filled with information on the surrounding country-side, its wayside inns, a ruined abbey that they passed.

"You love your Yorkshire, don't you?" she re-marked, after they'd stopped for coffee, then paused to admire the view over a valley where each shade of green vied for richness with its neighbor.

"I love it more with the right person at my side. It's many a long year since I wanted to share all this—and other things that matter."

Jay was astonished. Had he and Sheila Danby had so little in common? How had Rhys become involved with the girl if she couldn't appreciate the things that he valued? But she wouldn't inquire. Not today, perhaps not ever, unless she received some reassurance about his answer.

"No, Jay," he said, startling her by answering any-way. "There's been no one else who'd appreciate this. I know you, you see, so very well—from your love of art, from your interest in the changing scenery today, from your concern for saving an injured bird."

She smiled wryly, amused because something that had revealed an unsuspected facet of *his* character had proved equally illuminating about her own. Rhys smiled back. "Perhaps *my* brief anxiety for such a fragile creature proved that I wasn't, after all, quite so intimidating as you feared?"

Jay laughed and he squeezed her shoulders, pulling her against his side. "I'm glad you did find me some-

what off-putting at first. You had to be pretty determined to get through to me."

"You reckon I have then?" she asked lightly, but
already her heartbeat was pounding in her ears.

"Jay, Jay—do you have to ask?" A hand still on her
shoulder, he turned her to face him. Their eyes linked,
and held, as they did so frequently. His other hand
plunged into her hair, while he pressed her face against
his chest and, gentle as the caressing breeze, his lips
touched the crown of her head.

"We spoke some while ago of trust, and I hope I'm
capable of doing just that, Jay. I hope we can prove the
trust is mutual. I long to have this kind of day endure."

"Rhys . . ." Wonderingly, she stirred and gazed up
at him.

Although smiling, the look in his eyes was serious,
plumbing her own again. "That's all I ask of you, my
dear—trust, no matter what."

When Jay tried to speak, his lips prevented her,
sealing hers as though he sealed their future. He was
crushing her against him, oblivious of passing motorists
and of a lone shepherd high on the fells.

"Just for today, love, we are going to be happy,"
Rhys said eventually. "There is no past, no future, and
no one else exists. Every man should spend at least one
day, savoring the present, with his ideal companion."

Jay was so amazed that as they drove on she had to
say something. "You're not the same man I met that
first time at Scree Carr."

"And are you the same woman? Which of us remains
untouched by any encounter, however insignificant?
And I've never pretended ours *was* insignificant.
You're a disturbing influence, Jay Stanmer. I reckoned
with your shaking me up about those paintings, but not
with your effect on my entire life."

She didn't speak; she was too busy taking in what he

was saying, and all its implications. Rhys gave her a sideways glance. "So—I've admitted you're a current of fresh air to me, but you're not saying much. Reluctant to spoil my day by being frank?"

"Don't be an idiot," Jay said affectionately. "I'm just thinking maybe the niche I'd made in London wasn't either so secure or so satisfying as I'd thought."

"And your boss? You thought once that your relationship would extend to include your private life, didn't you?"

"I never—"

"No? Valentine talked, you know—quite readily, of what he hoped."

"Not when he was here?" There'd been no rapport between the two men.

Rhys laughed. "When I materialized in London, requesting your return. He was no more certain of my motives than I was myself, but he indicated that when he was ready to take a wife, you would be his choice."

"Paul had no right—"

"Ah."

Jay felt puzzled. Why was Rhys so interested in her reaction to Paul's assumption, when he himself had stated only the other night that he would remain uncommitted?

Rhys chuckled. "Okay, I've already broken the pledge to exclude everyone else. Blame the innate male vanity for wishing to remove all potential competition."

Sensing his real reason wasn't nearly so glib, warmth glowed through her.

At dusk, however, heading back to Scree Carr, Jay was dismayed to feel all delight draining from her. As the now-familiar moors darkened around them, she felt that their day's freedom was over.

Nearing the house, she heard a keening cry and glanced upward to see a solitary bird, another sea gull, the last rays of the dying sun tinging its wings the color of blood. Involuntarily, she shuddered.

"It's only a sea gull," Rhys teased, "not a vulture."

"Take no notice," she said hastily. "It just reminded me . . ."

"Of your first visit perhaps? Sea gulls often circle round during a storm. But was your introduction to me so very terrible, after all?"

"We've had this out already . . . you know it wasn't."

"And haven't you thought that that bird could be seeking refuge here? There are worse things than whatever menace you imagine lurks in my home."

"It isn't only me—you're not happy there."

"*Touché.* I knew we should have kept this our escapist day."

Although she had thoroughly enjoyed driving over the moors, visiting fishing villages along the coast, and walking hand in hand over the cliffs, Jay felt depressed the moment they entered the house, and Rhys seemed equally subdued.

They spent the evening in the lounge, whose warm cinnamon carpet and sofas in gold brocade made it one of the brighter rooms. But even some of the records Rhys selected seemed haunting—plaintive, restless, filling with disquiet the eerie shadows behind them in the room.

"We'll go out somewhere tomorrow afternoon," he promised before she went up to bed. "But I'm afraid I can't make a day of it, I've got to be at the hospital in the morning."

She smiled. "Okay, fine. I'll wash my hair while you're out."

As soon as she was in her room, Jay acknowledged that the arrangement seemed anything but fine. She'd have preferred to avoid the reminder that Rhys wasn't so well adjusted as he frequently appeared. He'd made no secret of the fact that today was an escape, a bit of pretend. Was she being an all-time idiot, thinking it was possible to overlook the very real problems here?

Rhys had been engaged. His fiancée had died and, whatever the cause, the very walls of his home had become saturated with gloom. Almost with evil. If she was to extend her stay at Scree Carr as she wished, she must somehow come to terms with its secrets.

Could she accept that she might never learn the full story of his love, nor the reason for his nightmares? Could she really trust him, as she must if either of them were to find happiness in any aspect of their relationship? And could she control the nervousness that had compelled her to switch on every light in her room, and was still making her so jumpy that she'd started just now when she glimpsed her own reflection in the mirrors?

Would she ever grow accustomed to the night sounds that plagued the place, so that the tapping of a branch on a pane or the sighing of the wind in ancient chimneys became a part of a spot grown dear—because it was *his* home? Or would she eventually wonder once again if Rhys had engineered Mrs. Godfrey's absence in order to have *her* alone with him for some sinister purpose of his own? Did she know him—or was she merely trying to believe he was the kind of man she admired?

It was no surprise that she slept only fitfully. Jay was thankful to see the dawn, and lay listening to the birds beyond her window, willing herself to think only of the afternoon and not of Rhys's appointment that morning.

She rose early, joined him for breakfast in the kitchen, and reminded herself that he appeared reassuringly relaxed.

He suggested they spend the afternoon in York, where they might visit the Minster, a museum that contained entire streets of old-world shops, and walk along the old city walls, if time allowed.

"It all sounds interesting; if there's such a lot to see, no doubt there'll be other visits," said Jay. "We needn't cram in everything today."

She realized that although the attraction between them was still as electric, even sitting like this over breakfast, they were also developing a friendship which promised to be lasting.

"I mustn't have bored you yet, anyway," Rhys said lightly. "Have you decided how long you can spend here?"

"Not yet. Did you want to know?"

"Stay as long as you wish. You know you're welcome. Have you contacted your boss yet?"

"No. I suppose I ought to, but Paul knows where I am. He can check."

After Rhys had left, she went up to her room and washed her hair. She was sitting brushing the tangles from it, by the window, when a dark car swung into the drive. The car parked too close to the house for her to see who got out. She heard its door slam, footsteps on the stone steps, and the sharp but melodic doorbell.

Presently the bell sounded again, stridently. Wondering why Amy Harper wasn't answering the door, Jay remembered she hadn't seen her today. Doubtless she had the day off. It seemed neither Travers, nor any of the staff, was in evidence near the front entrance, so Jay realized she'd better find out who the visitor was.

Jay checked a gasp when she found a uniformed policeman on the step.

"Good morning, madam," he began. "Is Mr. Felstead at home?"

"I'm afraid he isn't, he . . ." She paused, reluctant suddenly to discuss where Rhys had gone. "He's out."

"I see. Sergeant Harrison, madam. And you are . . . some relative perhaps?"

"No, I'm working here. I'm an art expert with a London gallery."

"Another," he muttered. "I understood Mr. Boxley was the art expert."

She smiled. "We both are. Look, sergeant, I'm sure Mr. Felstead would wish me to invite you in. Won't you come inside?"

She led the way to the lounge and indicated one of the exquisite armchairs, but he remained standing. Jay crossed to sit on a sofa.

"I can see why you're puzzled. Mr. Boxley and I are in the same line. Mr. Felstead invited us both to examine certain paintings."

"Very well, madam."

"Can I help at all? Or does this concern only Mr. Felstead?"

The officer smiled. "You could well be just the person. This is a routine inquiry, you understand, but I have a few questions. We had a call from our colleagues in the Metropolitan Police last night, trying to trace the whereabouts of Mr. Adam Boxley."

He took a notebook from his pocket, and flicked open a page.

"Evidently, Virginia Boxley reported her husband hadn't returned home. The lady became alarmed when she'd failed to contact him at the hotel in the village here."

"Would that have been the evening before last?"

"The twelfth. That's correct, madam."

"Yes, we knew, that is, Mr. Felstead and I knew she was trying to reach him. She rang through here as well, just before eleven."

"Seemingly, their little girl was taken bad, and she wanted her husband to cut short his stay."

"He was due to leave, anyway, yesterday. We assumed he'd gone."

"So neither you nor Mr. Felstead saw Mr. Boxley at all yesterday?"

"No. But we were out for the whole day."

"When did Mr. Boxley leave Scree Carr then, madam. Can you say?"

"Not precisely. We expected him to dine with us that evening. We waited dinner for some time, and he simply didn't arrive. Then, as I say, his wife telephoned, after the hotel had called trying to reach him."

"You say his original plan was to travel back to London yesterday?"

"Yes, definitely. He offered me a lift."

"Which you didn't accept?"

"There were some additional paintings I was to examine."

"I see." The sergeant paused, thinking. "Could you be more explicit about the reason for Mr. Felstead calling in two experts?"

"Briefly, I discovered that some paintings in his collection were forgeries. It's quite normal, in such circumstances, to seek a second opinion."

"And these pictures would have been more valuable had they been genuine?"

Jay suppressed a grin. "That's the general idea."

"Mr. Felstead wouldn't be pleased. And Mr. Boxley, was he worried perhaps about substantiating your verdict?"

"No. We do our job. We know it doesn't always make for popularity."

"And you were the one who broke the news to Mr. Felstead?"

"As I said, I was called in first. I didn't relish the task, but he's accepted my findings."

"Now they've found support," he said quickly.

Jay grinned. "Actually Rhys has since admitted that obtaining another opinion was merely . . . shall we say precautionary?"

Sergeant Harrison took out his pen. "And you are . . .?"

"Jay Stanmer."

"Would you mind supplying your home address—a formality, that's all, madam."

Jay gave it to him. The sergeant thanked her and began walking toward the hall. When he stopped on the other side of the doorway and turned, it seemed as though he'd had an afterthought.

"Did you say you were the last person to see Mr. Boxley before he left?"

"I didn't say, but I believe I could have been. We discussed our findings, and he mentioned his intention of driving home the next day."

"And nothing else?"

Jay remembered what Boxley had said about Sheila Danby, and kept silent about it. "I don't recollect anything."

"This, presumably, was inside the house?"

"We began talking indoors, then we continued our discussion out in the grounds. I think we both needed a bit of air."

Sergeant Harrison smiled grimly, and glanced around him. "Er, yes. I can imagine. Not exactly a cheery place, is it?"

"It's a lovely house."

He shrugged. "Not to my taste, I'm afraid, but there we are. About Mr. Boxley, can you recall what time it was when you separated?"

Jay paused, thinking. "That's tricky. It was late afternoon, but I don't remember looking at my watch."

After the policeman had thanked her for her help and driven away, Jay felt decidedly uneasy, afraid that

Rhys would be annoyed about the interview. Yet why should he be? He had nothing to conceal.

Alone again except for Mrs. Godfrey's nieces, who were cleaning somewhere on the far side of the house, Jay felt herself succumbing to the somber atmosphere. Then suddenly she was astonished by the sound of laughter.

She glanced out and saw one of the girls, racing from the vegetable garden. Giggling, the girl evaded a gardener's boy, ran through the kitchen, and then up the back stairs. She was singing now, lightheartedly; Jay realized how much the house needed laughter, and young voices.

She pictured Rhys, as he might have been—the father of a family, joking with them, teasing them—as all too rarely he teased *her*. Why had he needed to ask her to trust him *no matter what*, she wondered, perturbed.

Jay stifled a sigh and headed toward the kitchen. The two girls would have been instructed simply to attend to routine chores. In Mrs. Harper's absence, someone would have to prepare luncheon.

At last she heard the familiar purr of Rhys's car in the drive. Suddenly she felt all right, and hurried into the hall to welcome him.

He smiled instantly. "Don't say you've missed me!"

"Very much," she admitted frankly.

"Jay . . ." Still smiling, Rhys flung wide his arms.

Impulsively, she rushed the remaining few paces and was enveloped in a hug that extinguished her last scrap of apprehension. She could feel his heart hammering against her breast, and his quickening breath.

"God, it's good to have you here when I walk in. Is there no way I can keep you here?"

Jay glanced up and the longing in his expression made her kiss him. His lips caressed hers, tenderly at first, then more possessively, so that excitement spiraled deep inside her.

"You're a heady character to have around," he exclaimed. "I think we'd better compose ourselves and find something to eat."

"I hope you don't mind; I've prepared a snack. I wasn't certain what time you'd be in, so it's only cold food, but I found salad things and a joint of ham which I think Amy Harper cooked for us."

"She did indeed, I should have told you. But you've cóped very well without my intervention. Thanks, Jay, you make life easy."

She hoped he would continue to think so when she'd told him all that had transpired in her interview with Sergeant Harrison. Anxious to get the matter off her chest, she began to tell him while he carved the ham.

Rhys raised an eyebrow when he learned that Adam Boxley hadn't turned up in London, but he said nothing until she finished her account.

"What did I tell you?" he remarked wryly. "His wife is either accustomed to prolonged absences or has an overactive sense of suspicion."

"But the sergeant said that their child's illness was why she rang."

"Or the excuse she made," Rhys said, laughing. "Forget it, Jay. He'll turn up there, explain, and everyone will be satisfied."

The afternoon compensated for the troubled morning. Jay enjoyed their drive through the sunlit countryside. Although very aware of the tingling delight of being so close to Rhys, she also admired the expertise with which he handled the luxurious car.

She loved watching his long fingers on the wheel, being conscious of their strength and feeling well-cared-for because he was in charge. She could hardly believe he'd made her feel so uncomfortable during her first visit.

York was even more interesting than she'd expected. They lingered till the shadows lengthened and the evening breeze brought a chill to the air while they strolled beside the river. When Jay shivered as they walked along the ancient city walls, his arm went round her and he insisted on leaving.

"I intended to take you out for dinner tonight," he confided when they were in the Rolls Royce again. "But do you mind if I don't? I'd rather keep you to myself, and that won't happen in any restaurant or hotel."

"Of course I don't mind." Her heart began beating unsteadily; it was so unlike Rhys, as she once had known him, to admit to wishing to be alone with her.

"I don't expect you to cook; I shall delight in concocting one of my specialities. We'll open a couple of bottles of wine, and unwind."

"Sounds lovely!" She sighed contentedly. Was it possible that her desire to help him relax was working? Wasn't he increasingly seeking her company—and only hers?

Despite her happiness, Jay found she was more than a little on edge after they'd eaten that evening. Yet again, she was acutely aware of her need of him from the very depth of her being, too powerful to be dismissed, and alarmingly insistent.

As they sat, supposedly at ease, before the huge fireplace in the lounge, Jay wondered how Rhys felt. He couldn't be completely unaware of the attraction dancing across the small space between them with such force that she suspected it must be tangible.

Then all at once he smiled slightly and came to sit beside her on the sofa.

"Jay," he said, his voice husky, "do I need to tell you how I feel? How I wish that we had met before . . . well . . . a long time ago."

He kissed her throat, his tongue teasing its hollow, then his lips trailed a line of kisses toward her mouth. As her lips parted, she felt him caress her breast, making the tremor deep inside her intensify. She rejoiced in his need, and wished with all her heart that he wasn't so wary of the commitment that would have made her love him completely.

"Jay, Jay," he repeated hungrily, and his breathless kisses again devoured her mouth. She slid her arms around his shoulders, aching to draw even closer to him.

Presently, Rhys raised his lips from hers. "More wine, I think," he said, reaching toward the bottle.

"I don't know if I should."

He laughed. "You'd better! I've always been honest with you, Jay. I can't pretend that I'm unaffected by you."

"I know," she murmured, very conscious that Rhys was the one man she'd ever met whom she wouldn't—couldn't—say no to.

"Isn't it time you talked out whatever it is that's troubling you?" she asked when he'd refilled her glass. "Mightn't it help?"

After his initial surprise, his face hardened. "It wouldn't help *you.*"

"Don't you know I'd do anything I could for you?"

"That makes it all the harder, Jay, to do what I believe is best. For both of us."

"While I have no say in the matter? When I'm not even permitted to weigh the situation, because you refuse to confide?"

"Jay, my dear . . ." His dark eyes were so anxious that she stood up, facing him, her own eyes clouding.

"I know this is hard," Rhys said, his gaze continuing the appeal for her understanding. "You're accustomed to playing your role as friend, lover, or whatever—to the full, as an equal. I know you think I'm old-fashioned; in some ways I am. But that isn't the reason I'm keeping this from you. I ache to spill out the whole miserable story, only it could so easily spoil everything, destroy what there is between us."

Jay was about to question his right to make all the decisions, but Rhys took both her hands and drew her to him. He found her lips with his own again, his tongue plunging between her teeth, while the strength of his virile body awakened her every nerve ending. She leaned into him, concealing nothing of her own longing, deeply conscious that it was only a small portion of the love she felt. And, somehow, she felt if she loved him enough she would learn to accept whatever he wished.

Much later, though, going upstairs', Jay began to wonder if the undeniable passion that was drawing them together had made her drop all sense of caution. Wasn't she losing her head, as well as her heart, in believing whatever he said? Had she forgotten that Rhys could be using their mutual attraction to keep her with him unquestioningly? He had determined from the beginning to attract her; was this calculated to distract her from the things about him which generated misgivings?

Surprisingly, Jay slept soundly and long, and she awakened a little after seven to awareness that her dream of Rhys had left an enveloping glow of contentment. They had been together, here at Scree Carr, and although she hadn't known whether or not they were married, she'd been conscious that they were committed to each other, permanently. All her doubts of the previous evening had dispersed. She even smiled, as she went to bathe and dress, over the desire that had flared between them.

She still hadn't let Paul know that she was extending her stay here. Today she would contact him. And if he mentioned her taking over the New York gallery, she would admit that she'd reconsidered about going to America. Her time here had to end sometime and she'd have to work in London while Rhys remained in Yorkshire, but she couldn't contemplate having the Atlantic separate them.

Jay was on her way down to breakfast when a dreadful wailing reverberated through the house from somewhere to the rear. Looking for Rhys and Mrs. Harper, she hurried through the hall toward the kitchen.

They were both near the breakfast bar, their backs to her, making too much noise for Jay to tell what was going on. She saw that Rhys was pressing on Amy Harper's shoulder, forcing her to sit, and he was shouting while the woman was screeching hysterically.

"You've got to come, Mr. Felstead, you've got to!" Amy Harper cried. "It's horrible, horrible! You've got to do something!"

"For God's sake, Mrs. Harper, I will, I will! Just tell me what you've seen, and where. You'll only faint if you go out there again."

"It's a body, Mr. Felstead. By the path, as you come in from the village. You know, where there's all that bracken. I thought it was a tramp, you see, though I didn't see how he could have got past the lodge. I got off my bike and shouted to him to get up, that you wouldn't have him sleeping there. Only he didn't move, and then . . . then . . . I just touched him with my foot, and he sort of rolled over, down the slope. He's dead, dead!"

Rhys glanced over his shoulder. "Look after her, will you, Jay?"

He tore out through the kitchen door, which slammed to behind him.

"Oh, Miss Stanmer," Mrs. Harper groaned, "I do feel bad."

Half carrying her, Jay got Mrs. Harper to the downstairs bathroom where she was desperately sick. Eventually, Jay struggled back with her to the kitchen and began making a pot of tea, all the while keeping an anxious watch on the little woman.

"I'm giving you a hot drink," she said, soothingly. "Then we'll find you somewhere where you can have a long rest."

Mrs. Harper nodded, her distraught gaze flicking briefly toward Jay, then swinging away again as she stared into space, remembering, her entire face working.

"Try to think about something else, Mrs. Harper," Jay said gently, and knew how futile that was.

Rhys returned, his face devoid of all color, his eyes wary, as Jay was setting a cup and saucer on the table.

"It's him, isn't it, sir? That Mr. Boxley."

"Yes, I'm afraid it is."

Alarmed, Jay looked across at him. "Is he . . ."

Grimly, he nodded. "Very."

Mrs. Harper slid from the stool onto the tiled floor.

"You'd better call the police, Jay. I'll put her in one of the guest rooms."

Rhys took a couple of strides across the kitchen and scooped up Mrs. Harper as though she weighed no more than a child.

Chapter Seven

For hours there was no letup in the intense activity; the police came swiftly, arriving while Jay was at Rhys's side offering to settle Mrs. Harper. By the time the daily woman had opened her eyes and gratefully allowed Jay to loosen her high-buttoned dress and her apron, and then to slip off her shoes, they could hear questions being rapped at Rhys somewhere on the ground floor.

Then it was Jay's turn; she was conducted from the guest room to Rhys's study, where the interrogation was continuing.

"I am saying nothing further, Jay, until my lawyer arrives. You might follow my example," Rhys told her quickly, before the plain-clothes officer interrupted him.

"I'll handle this, thank you, Mr. Felstead," he said firmly, then turned to Jay. "Nethergate, the name is, madam, Chief Inspector Nethergate. Of course, you can choose to keep silent, for the present, but that won't help either yourself or us. All I'm trying to establish is when, and how, Mr. Boxley—if it *is* Mr. Boxley—died."

"I've told you it's Boxley," Rhys said tersely. Jay noticed a nerve flickering away, high in his cheek, and another at his temple.

"That will be established in due course," Chief Inspector Nethergate snapped. "Meanwhile, I'd be obliged if you'd permit me to ask what this young lady knows. I've no reason to think she might be connected with the incident, so where's the harm?"

Rhys sighed, his annoyance barely contained, and turned to gaze out of the window.

"I understand, Miss Stanmer, that Sergeant Harrison advised you that Mr. Boxley had been reported missing?"

"Yes, he did," she agreed.

"And you subsequently outlined what had happened when you last saw him."

Rhys turned and stared at her, his brooding, dark eyes furious, then swung away again.

"Mr. Felstead, here, has admitted that you were so concerned when Mr. Boxley didn't join you for dinner on May twelfth that you wanted to inform us of his disappearance."

"Well, I . . . was puzzled, because he'd been pretty definite about intending to stay for the meal. But then Rhys—Mr. Felstead—pointed out that he might simply have met someone . . ."

"*He* certainly wouldn't have wanted the police to come here."

Rhys stiffened, trying not to rise to the bait, but then he faced them. "What do you expect after your first, *unwarranted* intrusion?"

"To investigate reports that Miss Danby was in danger," the officer persisted calmly.

"Well, tell her what you found then—that I was trying to rid Sheila of her unhealthy obsession with that room, that she was the one screeching hysterically while I was trying to quiet her."

"Or to silence? It wasn't long afterward that she died . . ."

"One more word, Chief Inspector," said Rhys, his lips taut and his face gray, "and I'll sue."

Nethergate inhaled sharply, then turned to Jay. "Did Boxley have other acquaintances in the vicinity?"

"None that I know. I think Mr. Felstead believed he might have picked someone up."

"For a one night stand? Did Adam Boxley seem the kind of man who'd do that?"

"I was prepared to accept it was a possibility."

"Are you prepared to accept other notions, perhaps, simply because Mr. Felstead puts them forward?"

"You don't have to answer that, Jay," Rhys reminded her, without glancing in their direction.

The Chief Inspector suggested that they continue the discussion in another room. Disturbed, Jay agreed. Rhys was being difficult and obstructive. Evidently, he'd been annoyed by Nethergate in the past, but from the sound of it someone had been sufficiently alarmed by what was happening at Scree Carr to call in the police. And now it surely would be better for them if they cooperated fully with them.

Chief Inspector Nethergate smiled, appearing thankful when they were alone in the lounge, with the door closed behind them.

"You see, I don't even have anyone taking notes. This is quite informal. I'm afraid Mr. Felstead is adopting an unfortunate line," he said quietly. "I'm glad you understand that all we want is to reach our conclusions as swiftly, and as painlessly, as possible."

His questions were simple, seeking confirmation of what Jay had told them already, and yet when he left her, she remained upset. She couldn't help wondering how implicated Rhys had been in Sheila's death.

She was so alarmed that by the time they met in the kitchen for the luncheon that neither of them wanted, she was compelled to ask if he'd seen the Chief Inspector again.

"No, thank goodness."

"He seems to have put your back up."

Rhys shrugged. "He's agreed I'm entitled to have my lawyer present. He's in court right now, so until he's at liberty to come here, I shall tell that man no more than I have already."

"But if Adam has been murdered, they need all the help they can get."

"You appear to have obliged yesterday," Rhys retorted, "telling them all about my affairs."

"I didn't," she protested, feeling hurt as well as indignant. "I don't know what you mean."

"For God's sake, don't pretend!" His barely controlled temper slipped out of check. "They'll have recorded what you told them about those paintings, and anything else."

"I only answered one or two questions. All I said was—"

"Far too much! I thought I could rely on your loyalty."

"You can. I can't see what you're trying to conceal, or why you're so angry. The man's only doing his job."

"In a grossly offensive manner."

"But what have you got against him?" she persisted, still afraid that Rhys might know something about Boxley's death, and Sheila's.

"I should have thought that was obvious from what was said in front of you."

Throughout all the rest of the day, with its comings and goings of police, their doctor and photographers, Jay remained distressed by Rhys's reaction, which she was dreadfully afraid indicated that he knew far more than he hinted about the two unnatural deaths occurring here.

By the time his lawyer arrived and Rhys consented to complete his session with Chief Inspector Nethergate, Jay was feeling more upset about the possible extent of his involvement than she was about Boxley's murder. And *murder,* they'd been told, was evidently the crime they had to solve.

Jay's fears escalated. How serious was the knowledge that Rhys was concealing?

Undressing slowly that night, in the room which, without its winter fire, seemed very gloomy, she felt afraid even to attempt to sleep. She would be conscious of every eerie noise, and of the feeling she'd had, right from the beginning, that some kind of mystery permeated Scree Carr's very walls.

Alarming memories came rushing in, until the pressure threatened to burst. Rhys hadn't wanted her here originally, had he? He'd treated her as an intruder. What had he been trying to hide? And what had he wanted to keep from the police when they'd first come here?

There were altogether too many secrets and mysteries surrounding his home, too many deaths, too many *accidents.* How could she have forgotten, yet again, her own accident with the trap door? *After its hinges had been sawn through.*

She'd been frightened into running away then. Had she forgotten how scared she'd been? *Had Rhys made her forget?* Where was her common sense? How could she have returned here without demanding a satisfactory explanation of the incident? Was she so influenced by Rhys that it needed only one evening sitting together in a concert hall to make all her misgivings disappear? Was his caring all a sham to make her believe what he wanted, to keep her under his control?

"He can't want anything of me," Jay murmured, conscious of how he'd curtailed their lovemaking, and wondering now what other reason he could have for asking her to stay. Unless he knew that by keeping her here, he was keeping her silent. Boxley had been prevented from discussing those paintings. Would she also be stopped?

Tears slid down her cheeks as she slipped beneath the covers. Had it all been a fraud? Must she forget the rare moments of tenderness, the soaring passion, even the times when they'd seemed so well attuned? Was Rhys a liar, and a cheat, and—much worse than either—a murderer?

Dawn wasn't very far away when Jay fell asleep at last. It seemed only an hour or so later, although it was in fact ten o'clock, when a rap on her door awakened her.

"Come in," she called, expecting Mrs. Harper, whose determination had ensured that she'd taken charge again a few hours after finding the body.

When it was Rhys who walked in with a tray, Jay's emotions warred deep within her. Despite all the doubts and fears that flashed through her agitated mind, she could only smile back in response to his greeting, and feel thankful that he appeared far less unhappy than yesterday.

"I decided you needed sleep, my dear," he said, setting the tray on the bed. "I don't imagine you had a very good night, after that lot."

"I don't suppose any of us had. Isn't Mrs. Harper in today?"

"Oh, yes. She seems remarkably composed and insists on setting Mrs. Godfrey's nieces to giving the place a thorough polishing." He paused, and Jay reflected that he hardly appeared menacing.

"I'm not very practiced in the art of saying I'm sorry, Jay. But I was wrong to involve you in my long-standing antagonism toward Chief Inspector Nethergate. Instead of my own feelings, I should have been thinking of yours. Of the fact that because you're in my home you've been subjected to a horrifying shock, and an interrogation."

"Don't worry, Rhys."

He laughed, without humor. "You'll be as likely to stem the tide as that. But it is time you were given some explanation."

She reached for her cup and took a sip of coffee.

"You had a bad time as well yesterday. Explanations can wait."

He seemed confounded, and glanced despondently toward her. "And if I say I need to talk something out?"

She patted the edge of the bed, then took a slice of toast. "Make yourself comfortable. Incidentally, have you eaten?"

"Very early. I gave my lawyer a bed for the night. He had to drive to Leeds to be in court again today, hence my early start."

"And you don't want even another coffee?"

He shook his head. "But I'll guarantee needing one when I've finished." He paused. "You probably aren't aware, but I was once engaged. You may have known Sheila, the daughter of Sir Charles and Lady Danby."

"No, I . . . no."

"I suppose if you had, you'd have known all about it.

Sheila died, very suddenly," he said, his voice taut. Jay couldn't guess at his emotions. "Oh, you may as well know—it was suicide."

"I am sorry, Rhys." She was thankful she'd heard a part of it already and wasn't shocked into receiving the news in silence. But learning his fiancée's death was suicide was a nasty surprise. How could Rhys live with that?

"It was pretty harrowing," he continued. "All the worse because they wouldn't believe she'd killed herself. Her parents told the police they weren't satisfied. I don't blame them; *I* still can't accept that she had any real reason . . ." His voice trailed off. For a long time he sat motionless, his eyes averted from her, staring into space. He seemed to recollect himself, and indicated Jay's neglected breakfast. "I shouldn't have started this now, you're not eating."

"You've waited too long already, Rhys. I've been so worried since yesterday."

"It's one of the reasons I can't stand Nethergate. He interrogated me then. He's still convinced I killed her."

"Oh."

"And you heard what he said about a previous visit by the police, when some busybody here reported we were quarreling. True, we did have a lively relationship —sometimes explosive—but not without reason. Sheila had some curious ideas on how little being engaged should curtail her social whirl. And when she got something fixed in her mind, nothing could dislodge it. I don't take readily to anyone else being pigheaded. But since the police knew we argued, they refused to let that alone."

"And how—?" Jay began, then clammed up. She was so anxious to know how Sheila Danby had died that she'd almost asked, but she couldn't make Rhys relive it all.

His expression grim, he began telling her; irrespective of her need to know, he had to relate how it had happened.

"It was here, at Scree Carr, where it occurred," Rhys said stiffly, his fingers clenching. "I was too late to stop her."

"Oh, God!"

"I hoped I'd never see Nethergate again. He'll be all too ready to believe anything of me now."

She could say nothing. Any reassurance that the Chief Inspector would judge this death on the available facts would have sounded like a trite platitude.

Jay poured coffee from the pot into her own cup and handed it to him. "Drink that, love."

Rhys didn't speak again until the cup was empty and he set it down on the tray. The rattle of its saucer betrayed his unsteady hand.

"But the police went away last night, didn't they?" Jay said.

"Except for the guard that they left where Boxley was found, but they'll be back. Until they've sifted every scrap of potential evidence, they'll be here every day." He paused. "I advise you to return to London."

"No."

"Please. I don't want you involved. Go now, before the search intensifies."

Miserably, she shook her head. She couldn't leave him. While Rhys had been revealing the truth, sheer love for him had welled up from deep inside her.

"Think it over. I'm going across to the hospital now. It wasn't one of my days, but I can't just hang around here, waiting."

Without him, the day seemed interminable. Having learned more about Rhys's engagement, Jay thought she'd be glad of the opportunity to be alone for a while, to piece it all together and understand him better. But as soon as he'd left, Mrs. Harper came for the tray and kept her talking about the recent tragedy till Jay could think of nothing else. Yesterday, hearing in stages that Boxley was dead had softened the shock. Today, aware that a murder had been committed, here in Rhys's estate, she was hit by the brutality of the cold killing. Her dislike of Boxley was irrelevant and, indeed, made her feel more uncomfortable.

"You're worried about Mr. Felstead, aren't you, Miss Stanmer?" Mrs. Harper remarked, making her start. "He'll be all right. He's always all right at the hospital."

Jay didn't want a reminder of Rhys's apparent dependence on psychiatric help. She didn't want to consider that he'd been disturbed ever since his fiancée killed herself; that by his own confession he and Sheila Danby had argued. *Had* his temper flown out of control? Only yesterday, she herself had been shattered when he had turned on her. She couldn't pretend he was nearly so disciplined as she'd once believed.

The day was gloriously sunny, mocking her dejection and making her wonder how it would feel to live here with Rhys, sharing his love of the countless beautiful things in Scree Carr. All too readily, though, she recalled the other woman who had expected to live here. Rhys would never settle to life here with anyone else. Hadn't he said he wouldn't commit himself? Hadn't he more than once rejected her love?

Eventually, with real effort, Jay began to dress for the evening. To cheer herself, she slipped on a yellow dress.

Rhys came in early for dinner, making her realize that even today he could revive her sagging spirits. And he managed a smile when she told him that although the police had been around most of the day, they'd just seemed to be pursuing routine investigations.

"I'm going to have a quick shower," he announced. "See you shortly."

Before Rhys had reached the bend in the long staircase, Chief Inspector Nethergate came and requested a few more words with him.

"It's about the paintings, sir, the ones that Mr. Boxley came to examine."

"Yes?" Rhys sounded quite ready to give any information required.

"I understand they're likely to raise far less because of being fakes."

"Who told you that?" Rhys demanded, scowling.

"Miss Stanmer told Sergeant Harrison."

Rhys jerked his gaze toward Jay. If she had struck him, he couldn't have looked more injured.

"Miss Stanmer is quite correct, Chief Inspector," he said coldly. "Those paintings are virtually worthless. Anything else?"

"Thank you, sir, no. Nothing for the present."

"You have your motive now," Rhys murmured, turned, and ran upstairs.

Chief Inspector Nethergate caught Jay's eye and shrugged.

"Can I talk to you, Chief Inspector?" she asked quietly, shattered because something she had revealed could be used against Rhys.

"I wouldn't say anything, if I were you, Miss Stanmer. We'd have guessed anyway. He'd every reason to suppress your verdict, and Boxley's."

"But Rhys wouldn't—" she began earnestly.

"You keep out of it, eh?" Nethergate said as he passed her.

Jay wondered if he'd had second thoughts about

listening to her when the doorbell rang while she was still hovering, distraught, in the middle of the hall. She ran to open the door and stared, astonished.

"Paul!"

"Thank goodness you're all right!"

He strode in, seized her by both shoulders, and looked down into her face, his green eyes anxious. "I heard on the radio about Adam. I was already worried about you because you hadn't been in touch. I simply got into the car and . . . well, the rest's obvious."

"Oh, Paul. I'm perfectly all right, but we're having a dreadful time. I was going to ring you, the day Adam was found. Yesterday."

"Then why the hell didn't you? You should have phoned long ago."

"I'm sorry."

"Was there some trouble? Didn't Adam agree with your conclusions?"

"There was no problem. He could see that the paintings weren't genuine."

"Then what kept you?"

Jay just stared at him. What could she say? How could she explain that she believed she was in love with Rhys, that she couldn't leave him?

"You're coming back with me, now. We can talk *en route*."

"No, Paul." The possibility of going away from here was sickening.

"Jay?" He glanced around. "Where can we talk? Not here, we don't know who's listening." He looked beyond her, toward the lounge.

"Not in there, I think the police are in occupation again."

"The dining room?"

As she followed him through the door, Jay shivered.

She hadn't noticed the clouds gathering above the moors, obliterating the sunlight. Despair seemed to hang in the atmosphere of the darkening room.

Paul indicated one of the armchairs over near the empty fireplace, but Jay remained standing. She felt as if Paul were a stranger, because he didn't—*couldn't* understand what she felt for Rhys.

"Jay, listen to me. I want you in New York, by the end of this week. You need to prove yourself there, then we'll talk seriously about our future."

"Paul, no. I can't do it, not any longer."

"Can't? You're out of your mind! I must tell you I've had grave reservations about your suitability for the American gallery, after the irresponsible way you've behaved, just staying on here without letting me know. But I decided that I had to consider what was best for you, and that is restoring the Jay Stanmer that I know—the capable career woman."

"I'm not sure she exists."

"Well, I am. Aren't I demonstrating my belief in you? It's only that you've been out here too long. Once you're back in London . . ."

Jay sighed, closing her eyes. She wasn't getting through to him. "Paul, give me a little while, *please.* Just a few days. I have some holiday due, let me take it, now."

"You can't want to stay here." He paused. "You're utterly infatuated with Felstead, aren't you?"

"No." It never had been infatuation; life would be a lot easier if it had.

Jay glanced around them. In the unnaturally early twilight, this room felt forbidding, its paneled walls stretching into the distance made her feel small, and afraid. Shadows blackened the somber wood, and she experienced a powerful urge to light all the candles—to reassure herself that she had been happy here, on other occasions, *with Rhys*. Now she was deeply conscious of the emptiness because of his absence. She shuddered, sensing that he could be taken away—from his home, from her. And that was why she had to stay; she couldn't desert Scree Carr, any more than she'd desert its owner.

"I'm not leaving," she announced firmly.

Paul looked bewildered.

"I'm sorry," she said. They'd been friends; he didn't deserve this. "I can't help this. But I don't believe I can ever go to New York."

"You're being a fool, Jay. Of course you'll go there, and make a success of the gallery for me. Then you'll know what an idiot you've been."

"I won't. If you can't let me wait then I'm quitting. If I have to choose between the job and all that Rhys and his home mean to me, there's no question which will win."

"Jay, it isn't only the job," Paul continued earnestly, his eyes growing tender. He drew her to him, kissing her fervently. The door opened. Over Paul's shoulder she saw Rhys, his expression unfathomable.

"Jay, I love you," Paul said breathlessly, his hands already working feverishly over her back. "I've always loved you. When we're married . . ."

Jay was aware only of Rhys striding out of the room. "Rhys!" she cried, desperately.

He either didn't hear, or chose to ignore her. She pushed Paul from her; by the time she was past him he might not have existed. "Rhys!" she called.

He was way above her already, taking the stairs three at a time. Jay swallowed, controlling her agitation. She had to think. She could see what Rhys had assumed. If she wanted to convince him that she didn't care about

Paul she had to act *now.* Even a half hour delay could be too long. The cold glint in his eyes had revealed that he wouldn't listen readily to anything she said.

He wasn't in his room. She checked the bathroom beyond, wasting irreplaceable seconds, before hurrying upstairs again, preparing to face him. To face that dreadful room which always made her feel inadequate.

Not daring to chance being kept out, she entered without knocking and, whatever the outcome of the day, she knew she'd never forget the anger implicit in his rigid back, which was to her.

Jay crossed away from him, toward the paintings stacked in a corner.

"How much do you reckon you'll get for these?" she asked, steadying her voice. "We'll have to think about what you're going to buy in their place."

When he didn't respond, she glanced toward him. He shrugged, as though indifferent to anything she said.

Jay took a deep breath. "Of course, replacing them will take time. I thought we might visit some of the dealers in Europe as well as in London. Whatever you wish, my time's yours . . ." her voice died.

Rhys turned to stare. He'd been toying with the spectacles which he'd removed earlier, and he thrust them on. They didn't conceal the cautious hope in his dark eyes. "Are you telling me something?" he asked, his tone flat.

Before she could answer, a door slammed somewhere at the front of the house, then a car door. The engine revved, and wheels squealed over the drive as a car accelerated away. Jay felt relief envelope her.

Rhys raised an eyebrow. "Is that what you were saying?"

Unable to speak, Jay nodded.

"But why . . . ?"

"You do ask some damn fool questions."

A hint of a smile hovered at his lips, yet he remained at the far side of the room. She smiled across, but Rhys didn't respond. "You did say you wanted my advice," Jay persisted. "Don't you fancy the idea of traveling together?"

He strode toward her, pulled her roughly against him, and kissed her urgently, hurting her lips against her teeth.

"Now who's being stupid?" he said at last, still hugging her. "If I'm free to go anywhere, Jay, there's no one I'd rather spend my time with. But you know my hours of freedom could easily be running short."

She sighed, felt tears rushing to her eyes, and disciplined them. Thank goodness, he would never know that she'd doubted him. "Yes, but even if the worst happens, they can prove nothing against you, because you didn't do it. When they eventually release you, I'll be here, waiting."

When Rhys said nothing, she wondered if she could have been wrong about the way he felt. Anxiously, she looked up at him. "Is there some reason why I mustn't? Am I wrong about what's going on between us?"

His smile was genuine, if melancholy. Then he kissed her again, so fiercely that she gasped, and the tip of his tongue savored her own. Jay quivered as longing darted through her when Rhys crushed her even nearer. She was surrendering all her fears and some of her worries to the sheer delight of being held there, absorbing the scent of the after-shave he used, when all too soon he spoke again, gravely.

"Unless I'm being singularly imperceptive, you've just thrown your job back at Valentine, together with . . . his more personal plans. There are limits, my dear, to what I can accept from you."

"There shouldn't be. If—" she began earnestly, and was interrupted.

"*If?* Ah, there we have it. Jay my love, *if* I could see beyond this one day and know that I'd be here, I'd ask that you wait for me. Instead, I face . . . whatever comes. You have to accept that I don't take where I cannot give."

His rejection of her support hurt like a physical slap. "You've thought it all out, have you? Without a moment's consideration of my feelings!"

Rhys seemed astounded. "I have thought, yes. At the time, I could endure it, because I thought you'd leave."

"Sometimes you're insufferable! You're so sure you can face anything alone. Yet you want to send me away, in case I feel anxious!"

"*Want?*" Rhys interrupted. "Never!"

"Then I'm staying."

To her surprise, he nodded. She felt his enormous sigh of relief. He smiled as he looked down at her. Briefly, she felt an affectionate hand on her hair. "Well, I did try," he said. "Let's hope you never wish I'd tried harder."

"I shan't. I'm absolutely certain I'm doing the right thing."

"Jay." He gathered her to him again, and his lips traced hers tantalizingly, before they took possession in a kiss so deep that he finally convinced her that he truly wanted her with him.

Jay clung, her body stirring as every nerve awakened to him. She felt his fingers at her breast. His kisses intensified, and she felt the insistent pressure of his body against her own. She became conscious of the pillar of the four-poster bed at her back as Rhys imprisoned her there, as if to ensure there'd be no escaping the strength of his need. But how could he even imagine she could bear to move away? She was alive as never before, her veins pounding, as fierce as the waterfall that she could hear, and just as powerful. Surely now they belonged together.

His hand slid sensuously from her breast, down over her waist, until his sensitive fingers traced her hip. Jay sighed ecstatically, wondering at the delight which she'd never suspected would awaken at a touch. And then, abruptly, Rhys stopped himself.

"Not now," he said gruffly, "nor in here."

Horrified, Jay gasped. Had he stopped because this was the room he'd made love to Sheila Danby in?

"You still love her, don't you?" She couldn't believe that the happiness he'd been generating could be shattered so cruelly.

"No, Jay. I don't believe I ever did."

She felt wretched. "No? Oh, come on, Rhys, be honest. You've kept this place like–like a shrine."

"You're entirely mistaken. In fact, I put these pictures in here so I could make a new beginning—with *you*. Only that changes none of the facts. The police are still waiting. I am not going to do anything to make you feel committed."

She sighed, resting her head against him, unable to think, scarcely able to feel anything, except for the great need to be his. "Haven't you considered you might be being cruel? Needlessly so?"

"Only to *you?*" Rhys asked.

Turning hastily away from her, he ran a hand over his hair, but when he reached for the door handle, Jay saw that his fingers shook, and understood that he found the denial no easier.

"Rhys . . ."

He turned. She could see he was just as reluctant to part.

"My dear," he said quietly, "there's still too much about me that you don't know."

Jay managed a smile. "Then start talking."

Rhys glanced involuntarily toward the boarded windows, then stood with his back to them as, beginning to relax already, he started speaking.

Chapter Eight

"We became acquainted through those paintings. Sir Charles and Lady Danby were friends of my parents. I'd kept in touch after I was left on my own here."

Jay made a mental note to ask Rhys what had become of his own parents.

"Sheila returned to this country when her mother was ill. We'd met, years ago, but I hardly knew her. She knew of my collection, though, and tried to sell me those pictures—she'd acquired them in Paris."

"*Sell?* I understood they were a gift."

"So they were, eventually. At first, however, Sheila was looking for a buyer; only I wasn't interested."

"You didn't suspect then that they might be faked?"

"Not at all. But even though each was supposedly a lesser work by that particular artist, they would still command a high price. I could have bought the lot, but I'd no wish to tie up my capital to that extent."

"Then why didn't she sell them elsewhere or just sell one or two to you?"

Rhys smiled, but there was no humor in his weary eyes.

"Frankly, attraction sparked between us, instantly. I'd no reason to be circumspect. I was free of all ties, looking for someone who'd make Scree Carr a home again. I forgot the paintings; for weeks, I didn't think coherently."

Jay couldn't help wishing she'd had this effect upon him. "She must have been very beautiful."

"Is a butterfly, a kingfisher—a dramatic sunset? Sheila was vibrant, colorful, very exciting. This house fascinated her. She pestered me for its legends, hurrying from room to room, enchanting me."

"And you fell in love."

"Love?" He shrugged, dismissively. "No man could have been immune. Her hair and eyes were as dark as the rooks swooping about Scree Carr. She dressed exotically, jewel-bright." His eyes veiled. "While her mother was ill, Sheila came here daily. I was delighted when she responded to me."

Jay quelled a sharp breath. She was tempted to ask if they'd been lovers, but she didn't want to know the answer.

"When Lady Danby began recovering, Sheila and I announced our engagement. She used to stay here; intrigued by the story of the Felstead bride, she insisted on sleeping in this room. You're not surprised, are you?"

Jay shook her head.

"I never understood why she felt such an affinity. Eugenie had come here to a marriage arranged because of her wealth, yet sheer desire drove us along, *unthinking*. Though there seemed no parallel, Sheila's vivacity began slipping, revealing a darker side, though it was equally dramatic."

Rhys sighed. "When she admitted trying to sell me the paintings because she needed the money, I was incredulous. She'd had a good job, modeling in Paris, and I thought surely she'd have an allowance from Sir Charles."

"But you wouldn't care whether or not she had any money."

He raised an eyebrow. "I'm glad you understand. I offered to pick up the tab for anything she wanted to buy, clothes for the honeymoon, jewelry, whatever."

"But she wasn't grateful?"

"Anything but! She wasn't receiving an allowance from Sir Charles because he *wasn't* her father. I was astonished, but not more than that, because I really didn't care who she was. Again, Sheila made an issue of it, calling herself a bastard."

"Who is her father then?"

"I don't know. But I'd have given her a background —my own."

"That would have been enough for most women."

"Oh, come now. It wouldn't be enough for you. You're too self-sufficient."

"I'm not 'most' women," Jay said, feeling sad that he hadn't recognized that the independence was sacrificed already.

Rhys glanced toward her, looking thoughtful. "True —you're not. But Sheila was always particularly reluctant to be tied, in any way. However, she'd decided to give me those pictures on our marriage."

Briefly, he fell silent. "I thought to boost her morale by having them valued. To convince her she'd recognized a good investment and was contributing to the total value of everything in the house."

"And she was so scared of the truth emerging that she committed suicide?"

"I've been willing to believe that alternative to supposing any escape was preferable to marriage to me!"

"Oh, Rhys!"

"I'll admit that didn't quite coincide with my normal arrogance!"

"But would she end it all to avoid those forgeries being discovered? Can't you find out more about them?"

"I've contacted Christie's, Sotheby's, your company, Boxley's. Every reliable source, here and abroad. Most dealers learn of suspected fakes, and where they are, but these appeared as if from nowhere. If I unleash them on the market, there's going to be quite a stir."

Rhys checked himself again, and sighed. "I wish I felt I'd the right to ask you to bear with me, Jay; there's so much to work out."

She managed a smile, crossing to the door. "You don't need to ask, Rhys."

Briefly, his hand touched her shoulder and she felt as if, leaving that dreadful room, they were relinquishing some problems. If Rhys wished her to bear with him, they'd come out the other side all right.

Far below them in the hall another door opened.

"Is that you, Mr. Felstead?" Chief Inspector Nethergate called.

His expression grim, Rhys looked at Jay. "You see, right on cue."

He turned and hurried briskly down the long staircase. Jay stood in the shadows of the upper landing, trembling as she gazed over the balustrade toward the Chief Inspector waiting in the arc of the one lamp shining in the hall. Within moments, Rhys joined him.

By the time they'd completed their short conversation, Jay was descending the last few steps.

Without any words, something told her. There was no shock when Rhys approached, his dark eyes grave. He took her hand in both of his own.

"Take good care of yourself, Jay. I . . . I've got to go now."

"We'll allow you a few minutes in private, Mr. Felstead," Nethergate said, his voice unexpectedly sympathetic.

Impatiently, Rhys shook his head. "We've nothing to conceal. You know now, Jay, why it had to be no." His hands were crushing her fingers, grinding the bones together. He was struggling to contain his thoughts, but suddenly they emerged. "Whatever the outcome, be certain that I need you."

"And I you—oh, so very much."

She kissed him full on the mouth, willing him to comprehend the strength and the extent of her love, willing its power to hold them together through whatever separation lay ahead.

"I'll be here when you come home," she reminded him.

"You could have a long wait. You know the crime is murder, that while there's the least fragment of doubt they won't release me." His brown eyes fastened on hers, tying her to him.

"I know all that, Rhys. I know it couldn't have been you."

"I shan't forget," he said quietly.

His hold on her hand slackened, and she felt his fingers caressing hers, a gesture more affectionate than a kiss, more poignant than any sigh. "Thanks, Jay, for everything."

He glanced toward the Chief Inspector. "Is it all right

to telephone my farm manager? I need to give him a few instructions, since I shan't be just the other end of the line if anything crops up."

Jay couldn't take much more. While Rhys had his back to her, she ran upstairs to her room and closed the door. Yet she could still hear him, hastily gathering together a few things from the room across the landing. She locked herself in her bathroom then, and turned on the shower to drown out every sound. If she listened to Rhys being driven away, she would hear nothing else throughout the long night, through any of the nights which might have to be endured before the charge was withdrawn.

Jay couldn't eat when Mrs. Harper, red-eyed, called her to the meal that she'd been preparing when Rhys was taken away. Although Jay had told Rhys of her belief in his innocence, in her own heart she was deeply conscious that, earlier, even she had mistrusted him.

"What will you do, Miss Stanmer?" Mrs. Harper inquired anxiously.

"I'll stay here, so I'll be waiting when Mr. Felstead is released," Jay said, and saw that, after her momentary surprise, the woman was glad.

"I've telephoned Mrs. Godfrey," Mrs. Harper said. "I wondered if she'd come back to Scree Carr now the master isn't in charge, but he's asked her to see to so much in the London flat."

"I'm sure Mrs. Godfrey's right to stay. If anything arises here that you feel you can't deal with, I'll try to help."

Mrs. Harper smiled, and her tear-stained face began to look more like her old self. "That's good. I know you like the master and will do what's best."

"Like him?" Jay echoed softly. "I love him, Mrs. Harper."

"There, I knew it! I said to my hubby only the other day that ever since you'd come here things have been different. If this awful bother could be settled, Mr. Felstead would be happy, as he never was before."

"Never? You mean since his fiancée died."

"Since before that."

Behind them a window rattled. Mrs. Harper glanced over her shoulder, then smiled again.

"Maybe he'll get these window frames attended to soon. I don't think he could be bothered, just for himself. And while she was around he was too busy watching she didn't go off with somebody else. She changed everything, you know. It was as if she spoiled Scree Carr for him. There was something sinister about the place, even before she died. She was a selfish girl, as well, flighty, though he could never do enough for her."

Jay tried to smile. "Aren't you exaggerating a little perhaps? It's all too easy, after a tragedy, to read more into the atmosphere than there was before it occurred."

"Oh, yes? Well, don't tell me she wasn't plotting to hook him, from the start. She came here like something out of a fashion magazine with her low-cut dresses, and them flashing eyes."

Despite the traumatic events of the day, Jay was compelled to grin. "I gather you didn't like Sheila Danby, Mrs. Harper. Shall we just accept that, and let her rest? We need to put the past behind and work on the present."

"You mean, so if Mr. Felstead comes home, we'll have the place more cheerful?"

"*When,* not if, Mrs. Harper, otherwise you've got the message."

Alone, Jay glanced around again; the room felt just as forbidding as it had while she was with Paul. It was one thing to talk about fixing up the house, quite another to consider that *she* must make any improvements.

Jay sighed. She'd had enough for one day, and yet with Rhys being questioned by the police, she would find no peace anywhere.

Upstairs, she wandered, uneasily active, glancing about, trying to take some interest in the paintings which had seemed so fascinating on first acquaintance. Now they, like the huge tapestry, appeared curiously dead.

The clock was making an infernal din, ruthlessly measuring the seconds, as if some unseen being gloated over time elapsing. Time during which Rhys would be suffering. She couldn't get him out of her mind, yet that couldn't help him. Her own uselessness became a sharp, physical pain.

The telephone rang down in the hall and Mrs. Harper answered it.

"Miss Stanmer," she called. Jay's heart soared, as she imagined Rhys ringing to tell of his release, but Mrs. Harper's expression told her there was no such news.

The caller was Paul, from a telephone box on the way to London. "Jay, don't hang up on me," he began urgently. "I have to talk. I can't let you quit like this. I've been thinking how much we've shared—"

"It's no good, Paul," she interrupted. "Nothing will make any difference. I can't leave Rhys. Even if he's tried, I'll stay somewhere near."

"Tried?" he said, bewildered.

Jay realized too late that he'd known nothing about police suspicions, and it would help no one to broadcast them.

"You mean they think he killed Adam Boxley? If I'd had the slightest idea they supposed anything of the kind, I wouldn't have left you there."

"You couldn't have persuaded me to leave, Paul. No one could."

Jay hung up, distressed because she'd failed to conceal what the police suspected. Assuring herself that it could in no way worsen Rhys's situation, she went slowly upstairs again.

That was the first terrible night. Unable to rest, Jay was acutely aware of every sound within the house and beyond it, and more aware still of the silence from the room across the landing. She had telephoned Rhys's lawyer, but he reported only that, so far, the police had proved nothing against Rhys. They still clung relentlessly to their assertion that he, and he alone, had sufficient motive for killing Adam Boxley.

Hope was slipping away. If either the lawyer or Rhys himself were able to establish his innocence, they'd have done so by now.

Despite her growing exhaustion, Jay lay sleepless, watching the moonlight tracing a pattern across the bed and winking back from the mirrors. Now the inexorable clock and the distant waterfall were the only sounds. At four in the morning Jay could stand the solitude no longer; in all her life, she'd never felt so alone, nor so inadequate.

Ready to scream with the frustration of doing nothing to help, she almost ran out of her bedroom, then hesitated, wondering where to go. There seemed nowhere in this great mansion of a place where she'd find comfort, except . . .

The door of his room opened at a touch. She slipped quietly inside, closed the door, and leaned against it, remembering so vividly that first occasion when she'd found Rhys in the throes of a nightmare.

She'd thought then that nothing could be worse than helplessly witnessing his agony, but what was he enduring now?

Jay controlled her imagination before it conjured up some stark little room, behind an implacable door. Swallowing, she walked toward the bed, then without thinking lay on top of the covers. The scent of his after-shave lingered on the pillow.

Suddenly she felt very close to Rhys, and reassured. Was Rhys also awake, staring at a scrap of that same sky? She willed her love to reach him.

Hearing the murmur of an electric clock, Jay glanced toward the bedside table. It was too dark to tell the time, but she noticed beside the clock a framed photograph—of a woman. She could discern neither the features nor the color of the hair, and she didn't wish to look. She could guess whose picture it was. Everyone knew the impact Sheila Danby had made. Why be surprised to find her photograph beside his bed?

It was no use continuing to fool herself that Rhys truly cared about *her.* He'd been absolutely enchanted with his fiancée. Wasn't it simply that Jay herself was too much in love to see the truth—that Rhys had merely turned to her, as any man might when he was alone and oppressed by too many problems?

She felt tears on her cheeks, and no longer possessed enough willpower to control them.

The voice came suddenly, as if from within her throbbing skull, his voice: "Run from me if you must. But not from life; that's no solution."

Jay gulped. That first time Rhys had thought to restrain her, his words hadn't been necessary, but now . . . ?

Whatever her own feelings, Rhys needed her. But how could she stay when every reminder of Sheila Danby hurt so much and made her long to escape?

Trapped in a situation where she couldn't express her feelings, Jay felt scared. Scared of life . . . ?

"Give me strength," she said, and sighed, wishing she knew how to endure.

She seemed to hear his voice again: "Running isn't like you, Jay."

She slept afterward, waking when the birds commenced their noisy chorus. Then she sighed, not opening her eyes, refusing to acknowledge the photograph. How on earth would she get through the day, and the next, until he returned? And how, in the future, could they find any happiness?

Hearing the lawn mower, she wondered if someone was up and about exceedingly early or if she'd slept late. Instinctively, she glanced at the clock. The photograph beside it was poor, black and white, but she might as well know how beautiful Sheila Danby had been, and face the fact.

Reaching toward the frame, Jay noticed the first thing that didn't add up. This woman was fair, yet his fiancée was supposed to have been as dark as the rooks.

Jay stared disbelievingly at the picture, recognizing her own face, knowing she'd seen this particular photograph innumerable times in catalogs issued by the gallery.

Tears filled her eyes again, joyful tears, because Rhys had framed this, had kept it by him, a part of her. She felt as though an enormous load had been lifted. Although this knowledge couldn't improve the situation for Rhys, it was a good omen. It gave her fresh heart; she could do anything now. She must slough off despair and think positively of their future; somehow, she'd be worthy of the man who cared enough for her to frame this poor likeness. And she would never again doubt him—the picture was more eloquent than any words.

Going toward the kitchen, Jay recalled that Mrs. Harper had taken the day off. After breakfast, Jay left the house where Mrs. Godfrey's nieces were again dealing with the rough work. It was time she learned something about his estate. She would find someone to introduce her to the farm manager. Meanwhile, she longed to tackle something difficult, as proof of her determination. She loathed Mike Travers, and was frightened by him, but today she'd force herself to be friendly. And she would go on being friendly toward the wretched man until she conquered her ridiculous apprehension of him.

She eventually located Travers in the garage, where the heavier gardening equipment was stored. He was obviously astounded, his blue eyes instantly challenging her.

"Yes?" he said tersely. "What do you want?"

Jay smiled. "I'm interested, that's all, Mr. Travers. You keep the grounds here in immaculate condition. I'd like to learn how."

"Oh? Do I need you to supervise, now *he's* away?"

Still smiling, Jay shook her head. "Anything but! I was wondering if you could use another pair of hands. I can tell a weed from a flower."

"I'd hate you to get them dirty. I've as much help as I need, and Mr. Felstead's authority to call in others if required."

Dismissed, Jay turned away, but she felt disappointed. Her desire to help had been genuine.

She remained out of doors, nevertheless, wandering through the fragrant rose garden, breathing deeply of the heady perfume, letting it pervade her mind and ease away the irrational fear Travers always gave her.

As she admired the lawns and their surrounding rhodo-
dendrons and azaleas, she reminded herself that the
man was a skilled gardener.

About half an hour later, Jay was crossing the lawn
surrounding the house when she heard a tractor approaching and was astonished when Mike Travers
halted. He grinned, looking quite amiable, for him.

"I don't suppose you've handled one of these, have
you?"

"A tractor? No, never."

"They're not all that difficult. You drive, don't you?
I've several men working today, clearing part of the
copse. If you could take over the tractor, we'd be all the
quicker loading logs onto the trailer."

It wasn't the kind of work that she'd envisaged, yet it
would keep her busy. If she went back to the house,
she'd only feel useless.

Jay smiled. "If you show me the controls, I'll be glad
to learn."

Travers smiled back, but even his humor seemed
somehow . . . *strange.*

"Right then, miss. Only you'd better change into
something that can't be spoiled."

She ran indoors, found jeans and a cotton blouse,
then followed the sound of the chain saw until she
reached the copse. When one of the men had shown
her how to drive the tractor, its trailer was loaded with
logs.

"That lot wants dumping behind the house," Travers
said. "You'll see there's a stack of wood for the fires.
The quickest way is left, onto the path here, then right
round the house. Keep to the paths, mind."

Taking several loads of timber to the house, Jay
enjoyed the morning. More so because she sensed that
Rhys would have laughed, in delight as much as

astonishment. Doing something practical around his estate was satisfying. She was disappointed when Travers said the next trailer load was the last and asked her to garage the tractor.

"Do you think I can manage that?" she asked dubiously.

Travers glowered angrily. "I thought you wanted to help."

"I do, only . . ." Jay quaked before the fury in his eyes. "Okay. I'll try."

"You ought to be able to cope; you put your car away all right."

"The garage doors open automatically, don't they?" He nodded, and Jay steeled herself to make an effort again. "Anything else I can do?"

Travers laughed sharply, as if at some amusing secret. "We'll see. I've got to attend to things here first."

After tipping the last of the wood onto the stack, she uncoupled the trailer, and drove the tractor the remaining few yards to the garages.

The door of the one where she'd found Travers earlier began rising as she drove toward it, and she smiled to herself, marveling at the ingenuity of the invention. Apparently some electronic device was activated without her assistance. She was still smiling as she started to maneuver the tractor through. Without warning, the door began descending again, swinging down rapidly while she was only halfway into the garage. Instinctively, she raised both hands, protecting her head, but powered by a strong mechanism the door was too heavy to hold.

Desperately, Jay struggled to check its descent, but managed only briefly to delay its closing. Her arms buckled under the thrust, and because she'd been leaning backward, when the door caught her it was a fierce blow on the back of her head.

The force of the impact sent the tractor hurtling forward into the garage, where it collided with the motorized lawn mower, ricocheted, and shot back again, thumping Jay's head into contact with the door a second time. A moment before she blacked out she heard something metallic rattle onto the concrete floor.

Chapter Nine

Jay couldn't have been unconscious for more than a few seconds, for when she opened her eyes a metal bar, gleaming in the semidarkness, was still rolling around on the floor.

Cautiously, she hauled herself up, hanging on to the tractor till her legs would support her, then gingerly she felt her way about seeking a light switch. She raised a tentative hand to her injuries. The lump on the back of her head was already the size of a hen's egg, and sticky with blood, but her neck ached most after the whiplash jerking of the tractor as it had jolted back and forth.

Breathing deeply, Jay controlled her instinctive alarm. At least she'd regained consciousness quickly, and she'd be able to walk to the house. First, though, she was going to investigate.

She sensed intuitively that this was another accident that hadn't been accidental. Surely any automatic door would have some device to prevent such a mishap.

The steel bar was lying directly beneath the contraption that controlled the door. Noticing friction marks on the metal, she realized it might have wedged the mechanism to prevent the door opening fully, or even to force it to shut before she was through. Bending to pick it up made her head ache abominably and, clutching the area that was pulsing, she turned away.

Jay didn't dare risk leaving by the same door. She hoped the smaller one connected to the house wasn't locked and luckily the handle turned easily. She stumbled through and along a corridor until she recognized the pantry adjoining the kitchen.

No one was about. She could hear a vacuum cleaner somewhere upstairs, and somebody singing tunelessly. She was relieved; until she had considered all implications of the incident, she didn't want to discuss it with anyone employed here. If she passed out again, though, there was nobody she could trust, except perhaps Mrs. Harper, who was taking the day off. Jay hurried toward the telephone and rang Dr. Milner.

The doctor wasn't deceived by her making light of what had happened. Her voice betrayed the shock which made steadying the receiver impossible. Learning she was hurt, he said he'd be there immediately.

"Why aren't you lying down?" were Henry Milner's first reproving words as she opened the door. "One glance in the mirror should have told you to!"

"I'm all right, really," Jay began, and was interrupted by his laugh.

"How dare you tell such lies, Miss Stanmer? You wouldn't have phoned me if you weren't worried. Allow me to judge how 'all right' you are."

As she led the way up to her room, he took hold of her shoulder. "What have you done to your neck? And is that blood in your hair?"

Jay winced as the doctor inspected the lump bisected by a gash.

"Who hit you?" he asked, following her into her room.

"The argument was with a garage door."

"But those doors have a fail-safe device. They couldn't possibly crash down on anyone."

"I thought they might have had a safety catch." She produced the steel bar. "Could this have jammed the mechanism, putting the thing out of action?"

"You suspect the door was tampered with?" Dr. Milner demanded, steadying her with one hand while he ran expert fingers over the top of her spine and up the muscles supporting her head. Although she flinched, Jay didn't experience the fierce pain that she'd anticipated.

"You've evidently escaped a severe whiplash injury. I'm going to clean and dress that head wound, while you tell me about it, everything."

Jay told him about offering to help Mike Travers, and how she'd enjoyed the morning. Then of her attempt to garage the tractor as requested.

"Lord," he exclaimed when she described the garage door closing. "That could have been lethal!"

"It reminded me of the other unexplained accident, my first time here."

"Surely Rhys investigated the reason that trap door gave way?"

"I don't know, I . . . didn't ask."

"Didn't it occur to you to wonder if that hadn't been accidental?"

Uncomfortably, Jay swallowed. "Actually, I went up to the room where I'd landed and . . ." She stopped, reluctant to reveal what she'd found.

"And?"

"I discovered brass filings, apparently from the hinges."

"You think they'd been sawn through?" he asked incredulously.

"I wondered if they had."

"Well, how did Rhys react when you told him?"

"I . . . didn't. I left, immediately, for London. It was only after I'd left that I realized that it couldn't have been Rhys, that he wouldn't have—"

"Then why the hell didn't you make him find out who was responsible?"

What could she say? What had it been really—embarrassment, distress, because she knew she'd misjudged him, and knew that *he* must know? A combination of the two, she supposed, along with the irrational longing to restore some kind of normal relationship, and the fact that anything she might say could destroy the fragile compatibility which had existed so briefly?

"Leaving that aside," Dr. Milner continued, "don't you think the same person might be involved? Or are you too incurious to wonder who?"

"I've an idea, but there's no motive. Mike Travers was indoors on the day of the first incident. I wouldn't be surprised if Rhys had asked him to put out the picture I was to examine. And it was Travers today who asked me to put away the tractor."

"Sounds conclusive—especially since Mike Travers fitted those electronic gadgets to the garages, as well as the controls for the gates."

"But Dr. Milner, why on earth would he want to injure me? Or anyone else . . ." She hesitated over voicing the suspicion that had been gnawing away inside her for days.

"Anyone else?" he echoed.

"There seems even less motive this time, but the

more I think about it the more sure I am that he might have killed Adam Boxley."

"*Travers?*"

"He was working near where I was walking with Adam Boxley that last afternoon. I scarcely noticed Travers at first. He was the other side of the hedge, trimming it. But he must have heard Adam confirming that the pictures we'd been examining were fakes."

Dr. Milner shook his head, puzzled as Jay herself was. "As you say, certain things point to him, yet with no apparent reason."

"I've been over and over the whole business in my mind, but Travers wouldn't even know those pictures were being investigated, much less care."

"Has Rhys ever told you the source of those particular paintings?"

"They were a gift, weren't they, from his fiancée."

He nodded. "So you do know of Sheila's existence."

"Yes. And I can't help wishing they'd never met." The words poured out; Jay couldn't stop them. "Even if she was unstable, she needn't have killed herself, need she, giving him nightmares, upsetting him so much that he has to have psychiatric help!"

"Help?" the doctor demanded, sounding more bewildered than ever.

"I've heard you say how vital his frequent hospital visits are."

Dr. Milner smiled. "You haven't discussed this with Rhys?"

"If I needed psychiatric care, I wouldn't want to talk about it. And besides—"

Sudden anger blazed in the doctor's eyes. "That's precisely the attitude that creates the stigma attached to the treatment of what is, after all, only another illness! I'm surprised at you, Miss Stanmer."

"I didn't mean it like that. I was upset for Rhys. I

don't consider there's anything shameful about needing that sort of help, but I couldn't add to the embarrassment of someone who felt that there was."

"Believe me, you'd have done the best thing possible if you'd raised the subject. Give it an airing as soon as you see him."

"How bad is he, Dr. Milner?" she asked, unable to continue without knowing.

"There's nothing wrong with Rhys. You're the one suffering delusions. But you should talk to him about it."

"You mean he's cured?" Jay asked, her spirits soaring.

"Stop questioning me, Miss Stanmer. Discussing any patient with you is unethical. And I don't like your attitude, either to mental instability or to Rhys Felstead. Are you implying he's capable of murder?"

"Of course not. I love Rhys."

He was startled, but presently he grinned. "Then you've a remarkable lack of communication between the pair of you. I'll grant Rhys isn't the most forthcoming of people, but you come a close second! For God's sake, Miss Stanmer, be the one person who accepts him as he is. We're wasting time. How long is it since your accident?"

"Half an hour, an hour, I'm no longer sure."

"So, Travers, if it was him, will have made himself scarce. Never mind, the police will know where to pick him up."

"How will they?"

"They've kept tabs on everyone who might have been involved in Adam Boxley's death. If you'd left the estate, you most likely would have been followed. The men coming to work here complain of being watched."

"But doesn't Travers live in one of the cottages?"

"He shares one with Manners, the lodge keeper, but

if you believe he'll be anywhere near Scree Carr, you're less skeptical than I am."

"I shouldn't have delayed you. We should have called the police immediately."

"I'll telephone on my way out. While you rest, young lady. I'm sure that's all you require, but if the pain should worsen don't hesitate to phone. Is Mrs. Godfrey still in London?"

"Yes."

"So, you'll be alone here. I'll get Amy Harper to sleep the night."

"There's no need, and she isn't in today, anyway."

"Hmm, well . . ." The doctor smiled. "Not certain I trust your judgment," he teased. "I'll have a chat with Amy. And don't forget—use that telephone if your condition deteriorates."

Jay had no difficulty settling to the physical rest that Dr. Milner recommended, and though her mind was still overactive, she was able finally to dismiss one long-standing dread. With Rhys away from the house, there wasn't any possibility that he'd been connected with her injury.

She was thankful and not at all surprised when Mrs. Harper arrived. The next morning Jay felt decidedly unwell; her head throbbed, and her arms were almost too weak to hold the coffee cup brought to her room.

Mrs. Harper was her attentive self, offering eggs and bacon, sausages, porridge. Jay accepted buttered toast, and eating that seemed like hard work. "I am all right, I only need to rest," she assured Rhys's daily woman when she suggested calling in Dr. Milner again.

Jay slept the morning away, awakening only when Mrs. Harper returned with a bowl of her delicious soup and freshly made rolls.

Afterward, she lay with her eyes half-closed, trying

not to think. Yesterday, believing Rhys would be exonerated, she'd experienced indescribable relief. But although Sergeant Harrison had questioned her, and examined the garage door, nearly twenty-four hours had passed without Mike Travers being located.

She felt too weighed down by apprehension concerning Rhys to get up. Even though it was daytime, the house itself felt even more forbidding than usual. Every creak of the old timber, each rattle of the windows, grated on raw nerves, reminding her of the many restles nights she'd spent here, and of Rhys's nightmares. How would he ever sleep soundly again if he wasn't cleared; how would *she* sleep?

The car in the drive startled her; she couldn't recognize its engine sound. Thinking it must be Dr. Milner's, she reached for her robe and slipped her arms into the sleeves as she crossed languidly to the window.

Jay was just in time to see an unfamiliar white sports car drive off. She shrugged and ambled listlessly back to the bed. What was the matter with her? She ought to be up, doing something, anything. Before she'd discarded the robe, someone knocked and her door opened immediately.

"Jay—"

Rhys came striding into the room. His dark eyes sought her face, traveled swiftly over her, seeking confirmation that she wasn't harmed, then found her eyes again when he reached her.

"Jay," he said again. And then, "Thank God!"

She was gathered to him. Closer than ever he held her, while his lips cherished her face and neck with gentle, loving kisses.

"You're free, you're free," she repeated over and over again. "You're safe."

When at last he relaxed his fierce hold of her and she

gazed up, desperate to learn how he'd come through the ordeal, her eyes blurred.

"Are you all right?" she asked, her voice husky.

"Are *you?*" Rhys asked, more urgently. "When he told me what had happened, I went through hell wondering if you were badly hurt."

"I'm fine now," she assured him quickly. "And you?"

He ignored her question. "It's all my fault. I can't forgive myself."

"For what?"

"I should have investigated that first incident when it occurred. It's no excuse, I know, but when I got Travers to clear up the mess, he told me he'd found a weak spot in the trap-door frame. He promised to repair it, and you seemed no worse. I certainly never suspected the accident might have been contrived."

"It doesn't matter, Rhys. Not now."

"It does to me."

"You've had enough to worry you."

Grimly, he smiled. "From the first time you came here! Like how ever would I persuade you to return."

"And today. Who told you I'd been hurt?"

"My lawyer, on the way home. He heard down at the station, but kept it from me until I was released. He must have known how I'd be insane with worry, how much I care . . . how I love you."

"Oh, Rhys."

"I do love you, Jay. I ought to have told you sooner, but I've never been very adept at using the word. After knowing Sheila, I doubted my own judgment."

He drew her against him again, kissing her fervently. Jay felt the flare of desire ignite inside her as his tongue traced her lips, inviting them to part. But all at once he pulled away slightly, gazing seriously into her eyes.

"I deserved all of this, you know."

"No, Rhys," Jay protested, hurt by his pallor, and the telltale signs of stress about his eyes and mouth.

"I needed it, Jay. Needed to have my freedom jeopardized to teach me how precious life has become, because of you."

She leaned her head against his chest, letting the words flow through her, warming away all lingering anxiety and dread. Again, she looked up at him.

"And you are really free now?" she asked, not quite daring to relax.

"Completely exonerated. They have the culprit, and he's making a confession."

"Is it someone we know?" she inquired carefully.

He nodded gravely. "Mike Travers."

"I thought it must be, but what did he hope to gain?"

"That, my love, is a very long story, I scarcely understand it myself. And it will keep, at least until I'm reassured you aren't seriously injured."

Jay smiled. "I've told you, I'm perfectly fit. Dr. Milner came here, gave me a thorough examination, and told me I only needed rest."

"Hasn't he been in today? How can he be sure there'll be no aftereffects, delayed shock, or—"

She was beginning to laugh away his anxiety when another knock at the door took Rhys away to answer it. Mrs. Harper stood on the threshold with a large tray.

"So that's where you are, sir. I heard you come in, but you disappeared before I could even say one word of welcome."

Rhys took the tray from her. "This says it admirably, Amy, in your inimitable fashion—practical as ever. Thank you very much, we shan't require anything further."

Mrs. Harper opened her mouth to speak, but Rhys smiled at her again and turned aside to set the tray on a table.

"With Mrs. Godfrey away, you must be very busy," he added quickly as he began closing the door.

Jay watched him turn the key in the lock. He grinned across at her. "I hope she'll understand and forgive. There could be advantages in owning a tiny bungalow, with no need of anyone to attend to its upkeep!"

"I'll pour the tea," Jay said, thankful suddenly for something to do. Since Rhys walked in, she'd been so elated that she couldn't keep still. He went to the window and gazed affectionately out over the gardens.

"You may as well sit," she said lightly, crossing to the table. "It won't all vanish, you know. Nor will I."

He smiled at her, looking long and hard, as if not quite able to accept that her words were true. Then he crossed and sank into a brocade armchair. His long-drawn-out sigh revealed how exhausted he was.

They sipped their tea and ate scones and jam in companionable peace. Everything else could wait. There would be time enough later for questioning him about Mike Travers; time enough indeed, for everything. There would be tomorrow, and the next day, and the next. Together.

The following morning Jay was awakened by the click of Rhys's door. It was a brilliant day, with the sun dazzling her as it glinted in the mirror hanging near the bed. It was the first morning she could recall that she hadn't woken with sickening apprehension gnawing at her stomach.

Yawning, she stretched, and smiled. Glancing toward the clock, she was astonished that it was only seven o'clock, and now she felt the all-too-familiar alarm stirring. Why was Rhys about so early? Couldn't he sleep?

Yesterday, after eventually convincing each other

that they were no worse for all that had happened, they'd spent the remainder of the day relaxing, glad simply to let go of all cares. Over dinner last night they'd spoken of a relaxed day again today.

Anxious about Rhys, Jay hurriedly slipped on her housecoat and ran downstairs. He was in the kitchen, talking cheerfully with Mrs. Harper while she served eggs and bacon. Seeing Jay, his smile widened, and he pushed back his chair, coming to her, concern in his dark eyes.

"You're supposed to be resting, love."

"And what about you?" she asked, searching his face for tension.

Rhys grinned, ruffling her hair affectionately.

"I'm fine. And with Mrs. Harper here to feed me, there's no need for you to fuss round me as well."

"But you're up so early."

"I know. I'm afraid I'd forgotten earlier what today is. I've got to go to the hospital. But I promise I'll keep the visit short."

Jay was perturbed. "Do you think you should? I shall be all right here. After all you've been through, surely your treatment's more essential than ever."

Behind Rhys, Mrs. Harper turned abruptly, almost running as she headed for the door.

"Treatment?" Rhys echoed, his expression inscrutable. Suddenly he flung back his head and laughed.

"I'm glad you think it's funny," Jay said softly. "I've been so worried about you. I don't see how you can treat it as a joke."

His lips twitching, Rhys poured coffee and set the cup before her.

"I know what you're imagining, Jay, and it couldn't be further from the truth."

"Oh?" She was beginning to realize that this tied in

with Dr. Milner's remarks. But if Rhys *hadn't* been receiving psychiatric care, why on earth had he let her believe he was?

"Before I guessed what you thought about my hospital visits, you'd indicated my behavior left a lot to be desired. Learning you doubted my sanity didn't do much for my self-esteem. Initially, I guess I wanted you to feel like a fool when the truth emerged. But it was tasteless, to say the least, to keep you in the dark after . . . well, once I knew your interest was very real."

"Then why did you?"

He looked uncomfortable for once. "I suppose I wanted you to recognize for yourself that I didn't need psychiatric help."

"Sorry I didn't oblige," Jay said quite sharply.

Rhys smiled at her and covered her hand with his own. "Is it that important? Now that you've convinced me of your love, *no matter what.*"

"But why are you always going there then, or aren't I to be told?"

"Idiot! We have no secrets. I work as a part-time assistant in occupational therapy."

"But *why?*"

"I studied psychology at university. Given the choice, I'd have practiced full time in some area of that field, but I couldn't. My father had no other heir, and his health was poor; someone had to take responsibility for this place."

"Rhys, love, I'm sorry."

"That I own Scree Carr? I'm not."

"You know I don't mean that. But I should never have even imagined that . . . well, you know."

He laughed again, dismissively. "I quickly learned over there how slight the distance is between those who need assistance in keeping things in balance, and those who don't.''

While Jay was digesting all that he'd said, Rhys smiled again.

"Is food for thought the only kind you want?" he inquired. "I think Mrs. Harper has tactfully left us to it. You'll probably find her in the pantry."

When Rhys returned from the hospital after lunch, Jay was in the garden, dozing over a book. He suggested they take a walk.

"I've never really shown you the estate, have I?"

As they strolled he talked of his parents, who had died some time ago, within months of each other. Jay recognized the isolation that she, herself, as an only child, had always experienced.

"I've often regretted having no one to share the burden of developing the estate as Father intended—to say nothing of having no one around at the end of a wearing day, when you're too exhausted to go out for company."

Slipping her hand into his, Jay smiled. "I know the feeling. When Mother was ill, and Father so far away in the States, I'd have sacrificed a lot to talk things out, or even just to talk."

"Did you say your parents had split up?"

"When I was a kid. I grew up wondering sometimes where I belonged."

"I'll have to teach you where that is." Rhys squeezed ⹁er hand.

She smiled again, happily. "You have. But now that you're talking, don't stop. Was your father the one who was interested in paintings?"

"In their *value*. He was a true Yorkshireman, he 'minded his brass.' Mother took the active interest in the Felstead collection. In innumerable ways you remind me of her. Born into our generation, she might have adopted a career very similar to your own, instead of being content to help here."

"Thank goodness, things weren't any different. There might have been no Rhys Felstead!"

He stopped walking and smiled down at her, pulling her against his side. "Today, I'll certainly endorse that sentiment."

Although he'd spoken lightly, Jay had to check her disquiet. Her heart felt full because of the loneliness he'd known, the nightmares, and his determination during those early days to remain self-sufficient. Was it only coincidence that they were nearing the rear of the house, where every window was boarded over? Involuntarily, she looked up and sighed.

"The night Sheila died, I saw her running out of the house," Rhys began, as if she'd asked him to explain. "At first, I didn't even think to stop her. We'd quarreled before and generally I'd been the one to win her round afterward. I should have known this quarrel was the last. By the time I realized what she intended, she was too far ahead of me. I was in that room upstairs, *her* room. I ran down all those wretched stairs and out the side door. She was almost out of sight already . . ."

He turned his back on the house and gestured in the opposite direction. "I reached the ravine, and the waterfall, just after she'd . . ." Sighing, he shrugged. "Somehow, I scrambled down to the foot of the cascade. She was stretched out across the rocks, bleeding, with her neck broken."

Swallowing hard, Jay tugged on his hand until they walked on again. But then she sensed he was looking at her and glanced up. His eyes were unclouded, very direct.

"That was one chapter, Jay. And it wasn't *ours*. We

have a whole sheaf of new pages, unwritten, waiting."
He smiled. "And I've quite a flair for planning."

She smiled back. "Like when you plotted to have me
return here?"

"Precisely. I'd sorted my priorities with my customary efficiency."

Jay laughed. "I've always sensed you had the power
to manipulate me! Learning I don't object too strongly
has been the surprise of a lifetime."

Rhys laughed with her. "I'll remember that. But for
starters I know you'll have to go away, if only briefly, to
London to tie up the loose ends."

"I know. I can't really just walk out on the gallery.
There are jobs there only I know about. And I suspect
that Paul will make a trip to New York himself, to set
up the new gallery."

"And you'll have to sell your apartment. Or is it
rented?"

"Sell it." She sighed. "Oh, Rhys, what if it takes
ages?"

She couldn't bear the prospect of having to remain in
London while the apartment was being sold. She didn't
want to live so far away from him.

"I've thought of that," he said quickly. "Put the flat
on the market, then come back here at once."

"But—"

"It's mortgaged? For once, the fact that I'm not
without funds is useful. I'll take care of the mortgage,
love, for as long as necessary."

"I'm not sure . . ."

He smiled affectionately. "I didn't suppose you
would be. Jay, have you any regrets that I got you to
come back here?"

"Of course I haven't."

"So do everything you need to and come home."

Jay felt warmed and well loved by his insistence that he wanted her at Scree Carr. It was *almost* all she'd ever dreamed of what life might be with Rhys, but he'd said nothing about marriage. And even though she knew he'd said he wouldn't commit himself, she couldn't help feeling disappointed. Silently, she reprimanded herself for being less of a realist than she'd believed. She knew, didn't she, that Rhys was the one man who could make her happy? Couldn't she let the fact that he wanted her be sufficient?

Chapter Ten

"I'd better start packing," Jay said reluctantly, later that week.

She'd telephoned the gallery and, learning that Paul was in New York, had spoken to him there. He'd been delighted she was returning to London, far less so when he heard she was limiting her time there.

She glanced across the breakfast table at Rhys. "You'll be at the hospital today, won't you?"

He nodded. "Delay your packing, Jay," he said at last, "come with me."

"Why? I'd only be in the way."

"You wouldn't be. It's a part of my life. Part you haven't seen."

"I can't sit in on private sessions."

"There aren't any on the agenda. I want to show you what occupational therapy can achieve."

Still, she hesitated, preferring to know nothing about

171

the place which had seemed to shield too many secrets about the man she loved.

"It'll be fine," Rhys assured her. "You'll scarcely be aware where you are. Most of the patients seem no different from you or me." His brown eyes glinted. "Well—no different from *you!*" he teased.

Dr. Milner was waiting inside the main building. He hurried them along a corridor before Jay could even glance around the old, rather beautiful, converted house.

"You're looking very fit, Miss Stanmer. Far better than I expected. I don't need to ask if you've recovered from your accident. And you, Rhys—the ordeal of the last few days seems to have had little effect."

Rhys exchanged a glance with Jay, then smiled at the doctor.

"I'd be a fool, wouldn't I, Henry, if I didn't respond to receiving a marvelous welcome home?"

"You would indeed, and a fool you're not. You should have stopped behaving like one weeks ago and let this lass get close to you!"

Jay tried not to choke on suppressed laughter. Suddenly Rhys grew serious and glanced at his friend.

"Jay will always be closer to me than anyone ever has been, and permanently, I hope." He found her gaze, his own very dark and magnetic, promising more . . . later.

Dr. Milner smiled. "As I'd hoped. And just remember, there's no harm in a little spontaneity. I'd hate your relationship to grow stale because you waited overlong."

"Was there something else, Henry?" Rhys inquired. "Or did you corner us here to improve our sex education?"

Dr. Milner instantly was grave. "I'm afraid this isn't just a social chat. Travers is asking for you, Rhys."

"Mike Travers—here? I can't do a thing to get him off the hook. He should know that. He's convinced the police that he did it; he's lucky he's been sent here instead of jail."

"Lucky? Perhaps. As his doctor, I was called to the station last night when he . . . went to pieces. He must talk it out, Rhys—with you. I needn't tell you how vital that can be."

"What's he claiming, that it all occurred during some moment of insanity? Surely there's no other explanation."

"There's an explanation, all right. You'd better hear it."

Jay gave Rhys's arm a gentle push. "Go on, darling, I'll wait here."

"No, Miss Stanmer," the doctor contradicted. "It concerns you as well."

Mike Travers was in an austere little room, with a male nurse sitting on the other side of the table. Seeing Rhys, the nurse prepared to leave.

"I'll be outside the door, Mr. Felstead."

"There's no need," Rhys said quickly. "I know you're needed elsewhere. I'll ring when I'm through."

He sat on the corner of the table, nodded to Jay to take the vacant chair, and stopped the gardener as he attempted to rise.

"Stay where you are, Travers. Dr. Milner said you wanted a word."

"I didn't know you'd have her with you," Travers muttered.

"Miss Stanmer will be in on everything. We intend to marry."

Mike Travers jerked upright and glowered at Rhys. "Oh—it's her now, is it, that's in favor?"

Rhys glared back. "What's that to you?" he demanded, then sighed. "We won't argue about it. I thought you'd something to say."

"Yes. You must think I've no right to be interested in what you do. It's too late now, anyway, for anything any different. It was the shock, though, that made me snap."

"While we're getting apologies out of the way, I'd have thought you owed another to Miss Stanmer."

"I'm not normally violent, miss," Travers began, but his gaze, shifting about the room, was still menacing. "If there'd been any other way, I'd not have tampered with the trap door, nor with the garage. I had to stop you, just as I had to stop that Boxley fellow . . ." He seemed to recollect how much he was revealing and fell silent, staring down at his writhing hands, as though they were someone else's.

Before Jay could recover from her astonishment, he continued.

"I had to stop the truth getting out," he asserted passionately, glanced at Rhys, and then away again.

"What truth?" Rhys prompted quietly. "You want us to understand, don't you, Mike?"

"It's time somebody did. No one has. Do you realize what it's like when nobody cares?"

"The beginning's usually the best place to start," Rhys suggested, still quietly.

"Maybe, but that's not the hardest bit. I'll get the end done with."

After a very brief pause, Travers continued, "It was my paintings, you see. I couldn't let them find out they weren't genuine."

"Yours?" Rhys demanded, stunned.

"All seven." There could be no mistaking his pride.

"Are you telling me . . ." Rhys was incredulous. "Did you paint them?"

"You'd never have guessed, would you?" Travers said fiercely. "Not your old gardener, who only knows about cutting grass, spreading manure and transplanting. You never thought these hands could hold a brush, that these eyes could see more than lots of folk can see."

"No, Mike, I didn't."

"I could paint, and I could sell, only never sufficient to make a living. Until I tried painting like other artists, who'd made thousands at it, not a few pounds."

"Well," Rhys said slowly, "I'll grant you've a talent for copying style. But why?"

"I had to paint. That was all I could do," Travers said, as if anyone but an idiot should have understood.

"So that's where the paintings originated, but it doesn't explain how I got them."

"They were given to you, weren't they, *given*. By a bit of a girl who had a chip on her shoulder because you made her feel inferior! You had an immaculate background, hadn't you. And it was my fault that *she* hadn't."

"Yours?"

"Yes, mine," Travers said, his staring eyes challenging Rhys. "I'll always hate you, Rhys Felstead. By wanting her, you made Sheila forget everything she'd achieved. She couldn't believe it mattered that she'd made a good career for herself, that she was independent. Or that she'd learned to live with being illegitimate. She had to make you think she was someone special."

"She'd done that already, without much effort." Momentarily, Rhys's dark eyes sought Jay's gray ones; wordlessly, he asked her to forgive this reassertion of a fact.

"Then why didn't you make her understand?" Travers snarled, reminding Jay of a jungle cat with his barely curbed fury. "When she wanted to impress you, it had to be with something extraordinary."

"For God's sake, I'm not like that!"

"Aren't you?" Travers was shaking with anger—Jay could believe that his sanity might snap—but then his voice dropped abruptly. "Sheila never had much time for reasoning things out, had she? I suppose she gets that from me . . ."

"So, she was your daughter," Rhys said quickly.

"I've always been proud of Sheila, if less than proud of what I did to her mother. It couldn't have been easy for her, living with Charles Danby, while he was condescending to rear my child."

Rhys's surprise turned to sympathy. "I don't suppose it was very easy for you either."

"True, but it wasn't all bad. After we met in Paris and Sheila learned the truth, she was good to me. That girl *cared* . . . Why did she have to kill herself?"

"You're not the only one who wants to know."

"But you sent her over the top, by being what you are."

"Don't believe him, Rhys, it isn't true." Jay rushed to his side.

He took her hand, squeezed it, then let it go. "Sit down, Jay. We'll hear him out."

"My Sheila would have lived happily with almost any man. But not *you*, not in that mansion of a place, full of tales of brides that had died."

"She told you about the legend?"

"You got her obsessed with that Eugenie until I wondered if she could tell the difference between the woman's life and her own."

"She became obsessed herself," Rhys contradicted, "and for Christ's sake, *why?*"

"Can't you guess? That poor French lass couldn't

believe her bridegroom loved her. Did you . . . love Sheila?"

Rhys didn't reply. His eyes veiled, he moistened his lips, yet still he remained silent. Jay looked away. She ought to feel glad that he hadn't reasserted his love for Sheila Danby. She'd been longing to hear that he'd never been all that deeply involved, but all she could feel was sorry. Sorry for Rhys that he must acknowledge he'd never loved Sheila as much as she'd needed, and sorry too for the girl's father.

Travers' blue eyes accused Rhys again. "Couldn't you have helped her? Couldn't you have convinced her you wanted her for herself?"

"I tried," Rhys said heavily. "I'm not sure she wanted to listen. Half the time she didn't want to be tied down to me. She was here one minute, gone the next."

"She was too much like me," Travers said, shaking his head. "She was too hasty. And then she was in a panic. If people started investigating, it wouldn't just be the truth about those paintings that came out, but about me too. If she'd left it to me, I'd have gotten those pictures away somehow, even before I was working at Scree Carr."

"You took the job to get them?"

"To get *you.*" Travers's admission was all the more alarming for sounding so matter of fact.

"Why didn't she simply tell me they weren't genuine?" Rhys asked.

"She wanted you to think she'd given you something really valuable. I don't suppose you'd understand how important that was to her."

"Maybe not. I didn't realize what was going on. I guess everything together was too much for her—me, you, her mother, the paintings. I wish I'd known." Rhys sank onto the corner of the table again. "That night she threatened to burn them—said she had to be certain I only wanted *her.* I thought she was going to hurt herself. She'd have made a bonfire right there in her room if I hadn't stopped her."

"She always got riled up, just like me."

"I couldn't hear what she was yelling. She ran downstairs and out of the house still shouting, sobbing . . ."

"And you *let* her!" Travers leaped to his feet, overturning his chair. He threw himself at Rhys, his powerful hands clutching for his throat.

Jay sprang toward them, but already Rhys had fastened on to Travers's arms, forcing them outward.

"Ring the bell near the fireplace, Jay," Rhys said, glancing over his shoulder at her. "They'll come for him."

He looked back at Travers, who stood dejected. All the fight had gone out of him, and there was a look of weary acceptance on his face.

"I couldn't stop her, Mike. And you can't bring her back," Rhys said quietly. "Would you want to, if she'd feel as tormented as you sometimes do?"

After Travers was led away, Rhys stood for a while, staring into the middle distance. Jay ached to say something but couldn't trust herself to speak. Emotion was the last thing either of them needed.

Presently he moved, smoothed a hand over his hair, then removed his spectacles, polished and replaced them. He glanced at his watch.

"Let's find somewhere where I can be a bit of use . . ."

Rhys strode so briskly along the corridors that Jay succeeded in catching up with him only as he reached the rear extension, which housed the occupational therapy unit. He managed a sad smile as he opened the door. "It's over now, Jay. But I'm glad I talked to him."

Jay wasn't sure what to expect as they entered occupational therapy, but she was immediately delighted. The long room was bright and airy, with several large tables around which twenty or thirty patients were gathered. She felt Rhys's hand on her shoulder. "This way, love," he murmured as he led her to the far corner.

Jay smiled, noticing that the group here was concentrating on a large mural, which eventually would decorate one end of the room.

"My pet project," Rhys murmured.

"I can see that!"

Hearing his voice, the eight or nine people working on the mural turned. They surrounded Rhys—and Jay as well—tugging at his sleeve, or jostling to draw nearer. Rhys greeted each one, commenting and listening to what they had to say. When something resembling quiet settled, he explained that Jay had come to admire their work. They gradually returned to painting, but only resumed concentration when Rhys selected a paintbrush, grinned at Jay, and pointed to a chair. "Make yourself at home!"

Jay was both amazed and impressed seeing Rhys at work. Warmth seemed to emanate from him, and he could be both gentle and firm. It was a pleasure to watch him. She was surprised to find that the disturbance she had felt with Mike Travers was waning. Looking at Rhys, absorbed already, chatting to those around him as he deftly applied color, Jay felt profoundly thankful, even happy. The rest of the morning and the afternoon proved equally rewarding.

"Quite an experience," Jay observed, smiling, as they walked toward the car. "It was wonderful, Rhys!"

"Glad you think so." His arm tightening about her shoulders revealed his words as understated.

He surprised her and drove off in the opposite direction from his home. "I've had enough today, love—of Travers, his daughter, even of Scree Carr. Let's eat out somewhere quiet. Can't promise I'll scintillate, Jay, but I just want us to be together."

The restaurant was old, its interior plastered white with black oak beams and solid, well-polished furniture. Rhys was, indeed, quiet. Yet while Jay was recalling how he'd managed the difficult meeting with Mike Travers, she noticed his smile.

"Well, you've learned a bit more about me, haven't you?" he said. "Enough to make sense of the paradox I've become?"

"Oh, I think so," she responded swiftly.

He grinned. "And enough to make it impossible now for me to imbue my proposal with anything resembling romance!" He reached for her hand. "Marry me, Jay. I'd like to prove that all future surprises will be good ones."

Her fingers closed over his and she smiled at him. "There's no other way, is there? 'I just want us to be together,' you said—and that's what I want."

His dark gaze held on to hers, promising the kisses that must wait for a private place; promising the world . . .

The evening became enchanted with the simplest magic of all, that of needing only one person to be complete.

"I only regret that I didn't know," Rhys said as he drove back to Scree Carr. "I'd like to have understood about Sheila's father. And I'd have liked to have known that he was working on my estate."

"What difference would it have made?"

"Who can say? I'd like to think I'd have behaved

differently, given Sheila more self-assurance and, more recently, given Travers the comfort of knowing that, for a time, Sheila had been happy."

Rhys glanced at her when they arrived home. "Are you too tired for a walk?"

By the time they reached the ravine, Jay's eyes had adjusted sufficiently to the darkness to reveal that Rhys was thoughtful rather than upset.

"Reluctant to turn in?" she asked, closing the short distance between them to slide her hand through his arm. "Trying to delay the nightmares?"

"Not this time."

"We'll get used to them, you know."

"There'll be no need. You'll be close enough for me to be reassured."

"That's not the point, is it. Weren't they about Sheila . . . and this place?" Gazing toward the dark water far below them, she shuddered.

"Once, yes. They haven't been, not since Easter. And that's been worse, Jay. You see, it was your face I saw each time, *you* down there, on the rocks. I was afraid I couldn't care for anyone without destroying them."

"Oh, my dear . . ." As Jay glanced up, a cloud shifted and she saw that Rhys was smiling.

"You see how dynamically you changed everything. God forgive me that I was wary of loving you." He hugged her to him. "And you seem very much alive. I think that's another problem overcome."

The rain began, unnoticed, as they embraced. Soon it was drenching her summer dress, tracing rivulets through his hair and down inside his collar.

Rhys laughed. "There may be something elemental in our relationship, but it needn't have been endorsed quite this vehemently," he exclaimed, removing his jacket and putting it around her shoulders.

He smiled at her, kissed her full on the mouth, then seized her hand as they began running for the house.

Rhys was amused still as they trailed a saturated path up the staircase. But his expression softened at the door cf her room; he looked into her eyes again and squeezed her hand.

"Thank you, love, for today."

His lips caressed hers, making Jay very conscious of his reluctance to part, and as their kiss deepened and his tongue parted her lips, she found herself pressing involuntarily against him. She felt him glance over her head, toward his own door, and heard the faintest of sighs, which he tried to eliminate.

"You don't have to, Rhys."

"My dear Jay, I'm exhausted."

"And isn't that a part of it? If we're to marry, there'll be other nights, won't there, beside passionate ones?"

She watched the familiar lift of a dark eyebrow. "Who's the psychologist around here?" He pushed open the door. "Go along then. Get that wise young head into bed."

Jay slept in his arms, dreamlessly, stirring only once during the night, to contented awareness of Rhys sleeping beside her, his hand a caress against her hair.

When she awakened it was still dark, but although the bed was warm at her side, Rhys was no longer there. At first, she felt too contented to move but as she grew acutely conscious of rain lashing the windows, and the increased sighing of the wind, sleep was impossible.

Without warning, a tremendous clattering and crashing commenced, somewhere overhead. Alarmed, Jay sat upright, listening. If the noise had continued, Jay might have stayed where she was. But when silence fell, her imagination ran rampant. She couldn't bear not knowing any longer.

Hurriedly, she slipped her feet into her slippers and ran onto the landing.

Even in summer, the drafts penetrating the house were cool. Jay shivered, clutching her bare arms about her, wishing her nightgown were more substantial than thin straps supporting a wispy lace bodice. She ran upstairs to the room with the paintings.

As she entered she saw Rhys on a stepladder, reaching through the open window. He was tearing rapidly at the broken boarding, then tossing it toward a heap of wood growing in one corner.

As he glanced toward her and smiled, a gleam of early sun lit his face, making it glow with an intensity that seemed to match his eyes.

"Morning," he greeted her nonchalantly, and continued removing the rest of the timber.

Jay closed her eyes, relief flooding through her as she understood that, far from being upset, Rhys was happy. He closed the window, tossed the timber onto the pile, and walked toward her.

"Well?" he asked, and she noticed his exhilaration.

Jay could only gaze at him, wordlessly, smiling. He led her to the windows. Beyond the trees of the estate, a long, thin ribbon of light rested on the moors, silhouetting an isolated oak and a cluster of rocks.

"I've been waiting for the dawn," Rhys said, and looked down at her, drawing her hard against his side. He was excited. An answering quiver ran through Jay.

"Our children will have to learn that the waterfall must be treated with respect. But they'll have their own water. I'm going to build a swimming pool behind that line of beeches. It may be too cool to use it much here, but I want them to have everything, Jay."

Still smiling, she nodded. For once, she didn't quite know what to say. Rhys had surprised her again. It made her realize that much as she might want to understand him completely, she wouldn't wish away his complexity. In ten years, twenty, Rhys would still be surprising her. And maybe surprising himself.

"Rhys, I do love you!"

He held her to him. "Good." And then he laughed gently. "You've astonished me, Jay. I was afraid you'd think it was too soon for settling to domesticity. Where's the dedicated art expert?"

"Still around somewhere," she murmured, slipping her arms about him. "She'll be resurrected—when there's time."

"Meanwhile?" he prompted, mischief warming his brown eyes. "Now that I'm committed so completely, isn't it time you stopped resisting my powerful attraction?" he teased.

Jay smiled up at him. "With splinters of wood in your hair, scratches all over your hands, smudges on your face . . ."

"They're quickly remedied."

Impulsively grasping her hand, Rhys pulled her along with him as he began running down the stairs. He opened the door of his room and drew her slowly into his arms. "Jay, I do so need you!" he exclaimed, against her mouth. His slender fingers sought her breast, caressing her and engendering a fierce thrill of longing.

His tongue lingered over her lips, parting them, arousing her so that she returned his kisses hungrily, stirring, feeling him stir against her. He was alerting every nerve and she felt restored, alive again. She was exhilarated by his desire, aching to fulfill it, for at last neither of them would deny any part of their feelings for each other.

"Thank goodness, I installed showers here," Rhys murmured, his dark eyes glinting again as he gently released her. "They're very quick," he added, hurrying into the bathroom.

Over the splashing of the shower, he called to her again. "On second thought, Jay, you'd better come here."

Ridiculously, she hesitated, then smiled at herself. She was being a fool. Moments ago she'd been in Rhys's arms, committing herself entirely to him. Being unnerved by the prospect of seeing him naked didn't make sense. Yet still she paused in the bathroom doorway, feeling about sixteen, and totally inexperienced. The glass panel around the shower slid back.

"Darling?" he said, sounding puzzled. Drenched, his hair had started to curl, softening his features. He dashed water from his eyes, and she read there his tender amazement. "Jay, am I the first?"

She could not answer.

"Come here, love."

Slowly, she walked toward him. He was tinged with a lingering tan from the previous summer, gilded, glistening. The water swirled over his powerful shoulders, and traced in rivulets down his chest and flat stomach. He seemed very tall, his legs perfectly proportioned. She'd never thought a male body could be beautiful, yet alongside her undeniable desire was the awe she would feel for a perfect sculpture.

"Aren't you overdressed, Jay?"

Hastily, she glanced down, aware suddenly of her own body, wondering if he'd find her sufficiently alluring.

Rhys smiled, and reached above his head to lessen the force of the shower. "As you are then." He took her gently by the arm. "Come here."

She was drawn with him into the water. Rhys smiled again as, instantly, her nightgown was saturated.

"Mmm," he approved, "a subtle veiling for my bride."

As their bodies met he kissed her, eagerly, yet with the same tenderness she'd noticed earlier.

"I'll try to be considerate, my love," he whispered. "You've surprised me, you know. I'd thought . . ."

"That I was very much the sophisticated woman about town?"

"Do you think I'm not pleased? And thankful that we didn't rush headlong into something more deserving of regard," he added, his voice husky. "You've made me love, Jay, remember that. And remember desire's only a part of this . . ."

His mouth prevented her replying. She responded immediately, her arms slipping around his back as her lips parted yet again to welcome his probing tongue. She heard a moan and knew it was her own. As she leaned into the delicious pressure of his hard body, Rhys turned off the shower. Then, still holding her to him, he reached for a large towel.

For a long minute he gazed at her, breathing quickly, his eyes very dark. Then he smiled. Swiftly, he slid the drenched nightgown from her. Lowering his head, he kissed each breast in turn, and she was enveloped with him in the towel, held so closely that she could hardly breathe while his hands, warm through the toweling, blotted away moisture.

"I didn't know I was this patient," Rhys remarked, still smiling. "And I suspect it won't last."

Adroitly, he freed himself of the towel and, keeping her wrapped in its folds, carried her to the bed. He sat on its edge, looking like a virile Roman god, powerful and, perhaps, a little awesome. He tossed aside one edge of the towel, his eyes adoring her every curve. As he went to turn back the towel completely, his dark glance leveled with hers.

"Jay, Jay. I've waited so long!"

He kissed her repeatedly while his sensitive fingers sought her breast then the line of her hip, and afterward her leg. The pulsing, spreading and spiraling from deep inside her, was vibrating through every vein, urging her to respond. Her arms went round his shoulders, drawing him to her, then the fingers of one hand slid up into the damp hair at the nape of his neck.

"Hold me, Rhys, hold me . . ."

"Always."